David Stanley was born in Liverpool and is a father of 3 children. For 30 years he performed and penned lyrics and music for various local rock bands and, although his gigging career is over, his love for writing and letting his imagination run wild is still thriving inside.

Currently, he is a manager for Britain's largest train operating company.

Twitter@davidstanley147

GW00472376

I would like to dedicate this book to my children, especially my youngest daughter who must be glad that I have finished the book due to the numerous telephone calls I gave her when I was writing it, looking for guidance and inspiration. Sorry lovely but I am writing another one.

David Stanley

THE BAG

AUSTIN MACAULEY PUBLISHERS™

LONDON • CAMBRIDGE • NEW YORK • SHARJAH

A CIP catalogue record for this title is available from the British Library.

ISBN 9781786939951 (Paperback)
ISBN 9781786939968 (E-Book)
www.austinmacauley.com

First Published (2017)
Austin Macauley Publishers Ltd.
25 Canada Square
Canary Wharf
London
E14 5LQ

Acknowledgements

I'd like to thank *Liverpool Daily Post* and *Echo* for the use of their name within the book.

11th April

Shaun strolled along the old disused railway line that has now been converted into a cycle track and walking route with his trusty 10-year-old Jack Russell called Barney, memories of his father filling his mind as this is where his father walked his own dog, Bess. Bess was a big, black Labrador and for some strange reason used to like to chew the old ballast stones which used to keep the track in place and could still be found alongside the pathway.

Shaun himself looked after Bess for the last 2 years of her life due to the death of his father from prostate cancer. I guess it's rare for a Labrador to live to be nearly 19 years old, and Bess had a calming influence on Shaun for the last 2 years of her life as Bess gave him love and devotion at a time when he needed it most due to the breakup of his 1st marriage. He was letting his memories flow on but was stopped in his tracks when his own dog started barking at something in the bushes and tall grass. He went over to see what it was as Barney went scurrying through the tall grass like a lunatic, '*a rat I guess,*' he thought, but Barney kept on barking and then he noticed a large brown holdall bag in the tall grass, which looked damp but still looked kind of new.

He knew he had a big decision to make! Does he open the bag or just walk away from it? In work he could make big decisions, but when at home it took him ages to decide things such as: does he have toast on a morning or a just a biscuit? Normally the biscuit would always win as it took 3 minutes to make toast. But here and now his mind was in a quandary: open the bag or walk?! It was clear that a rat or something was trying to find out what the contents of the bag were too which only made his mind go into overdrive, maybe there is dead cat in there or even a dead dog in the bag! He looked around to see if anyone else was walking by, neither knowing why he was looking as it's not likely he would stop someone and say 'Hey! Shall I open this bag?' Barney returned to the bag and started sniffing around it, '*fuck it, let's open the thing*'. He stooped down to open the bag the way a cop would stoop slowly over a bomb to cut the red or blue wire and, gently taking the zip fastener, he started to open it and with his left hand he slightly pulled at the bag to feel for the weight in it, '*hmm, feels heavy,*' he thought before fully releasing the zip.

He opened the bag with dread, fearing the worst in case anything nasty was inside, but his eyes lit up as he realised he was looking at bundles of money.

'*Geez, jackpot!*' he thought, and as he moved the money around in the bag he then noticed a gun, '*shit this is real gangster stuff this, Christ, they may be coming back for it*'. His heart rate was now ticking over at a fast pace as the rush of adrenaline was starting to kick in, he lifted the bag but as he did he noticed something else about 4 feet away in the tall grass.

It was a body of a man. He was now starting to panic as never before and shouted at himself to calm down and went over to the body. The man was lying face down and, using his foot to roll the man's body over, the man's shirt was saturated in blood and by the way the body rolled over he must have been dead for a while as the body was quite stiff. He tried to think clearly as he was aware this was a fight or flight moment, once again he looked around him, studying the path for any passer-by, and picked up the bag then made large strides back to the opening where his car was parked in a nearby street. It was only about half a mile away from where the body and the bag lay but it seemed miles away as his mind went into overdrive, constantly looking out for people and shouting for Barney to keep up with him. On arrival at the path entrance he checked for any passing cars or people as the last thing he wanted was to be noticed carrying a big holdall bag. He walked around the corner to his car and as he fumbled in his pocket for his car keys he noticed a man who appeared to be fixing his garage roof, '*shit, hope he doesn't look my way,*' he thought.

He opened the boot of his car, threw the bag inside, opened the passenger door to let Barney in and quickly ran around the other side and got in the car. He looked all around him to see if anyone was looking and rolled up a cig, with difficulty as his hands was shaking, but as he lit the cig he could feel the calming effect of the nicotine instantly and as he pulled hard on the cig he scanned the area again and he could see the man on the garage roof who was still going about his day as normal. He fired up the engine and drove back towards his home, the traffic was just as heavy as normal but all he wanted to do was get back home and he could feel the frustration as he was stuck at the traffic lights.

He eventually arrived home and quickly opened the front door and got Barney inside. Walking straight to the kitchen to put the kettle on he said to himself, "A cup of tea definitely needed here", like the tea had some sort of answer to it all.

He made the brew and sat there trying to make sense of what has just happened and at the same time tried to understand why he simply didn't just call the police. This type of behaviour was totally alien to him as normally he was a very law abiding person, but for the few minutes on seeing the money in the bag he had seen the chance of being debt free and a new start in life and took it. As a lad, he was a wild card but always knew the boundaries, but loved the thrill and excitement of a chase and often, like many young lads, would like to imagine doing a big robbery like in the movies but he knew also that he wouldn't like going to prison, plus it was always going to be a fantasy as in truth he didn't have it in him to do such a thing, maybe it was his Catholic upbringing as he always throughout his life battled between good and bad. His only other thought candy was, again like millions of people throughout the world, winning the lotto, as the one weakness he had was money and he has spent most of his life spending more money than he had and couldn't save up money to save his life. He often wondered why he was like this and why he would also like to gamble at times, as he didn't need the money really, as he wasn't the type of person who needed flashy things, but maybe secretly somewhere deep down he wanted to try a new lifestyle. For just over a year now he had been living on his own and going through the motions of going to work and trying to fill his nights and days with various hobbies to keep his mind off his ex-wife and trying to mask the loneliness he felt inside.

He drank his tea and thought it would be best to wait for darkness to come around before he attempted to get the bag out of the car as he didn't want anyone seeing him. His mind then went back to the body of the man who was lying face down in the grass and saturated with blood. He wanted to call the police still as the idea of someone not at rest bothered him, though he felt it was only a matter of time before someone else discovered him. He somehow felt more relaxed now and carefully retraced his steps in his mind, he thought of maybe going back to the scene and calling the police as if he had only just stumbled across the body, but thought maybe this wasn't such a good idea as there may be more than just police wanting answers, '*I cannot call the police on a pay phone either as the police have cameras everywhere now and before you know it I will be on every local news channel saying "have you seen this man", think I will just wait a bit longer and let the night fall*'.

In the meantime, he kept the local radio station on, listening for any news of the body, and sat there and tried to work out some sort of plan to keep him safe and how to avoid suspicion. Out came a note pad and he scribbled:

1. Don't spend too much in one place

2. Don't place any large sums in the bank, maybe just small amounts every other week

3. Get rid of the gun

4. Live well happy

'*Simple enough plan*', he thought, '*just as long as no one seen me carrying that bloody big holdall bag across the path*', but he knew he would have to be serious to keep this a secret and would need more than a simple plan.

As nightfall approached there had been no news of the body and the anticipation of getting the bag out of the car was building, after yet another cup of tea and a ham sandwich he put the TV on as the local news was now due. As he reached over for his tobacco to make a roll up, the news he was waiting for got announced,

"A man's body has been found in the West Derby area of Liverpool, which we are led to believe was killed due to shotgun wounds and the police have not yet given any details of the body."

He sat there and thought that by now the police would be combing the area with police dogs and searching for clues and most likely asking every cyclist and dog walker who uses the path whether they heard or saw anything. '*I guess they have the area sealed off at the moment and have all the tents out, and likely to be for days so am going to give that area a miss for a while and Barney can go for a walk around the neighbourhood till it all settles down,*' he decided. His mind thought back to the body of the man and was glad that he had been found and can now be put to rest rather than let the rats gnaw at him any longer, just the worms next.

10 o'clock came around more slowly than other nights as he had been clock watching all afternoon and he put the TV back on again for News at 10 as they have a local news bulletin at the end of it for the North West when suddenly, just after a brief session of members of parliament trying to do their thing to be voted prime minister, the next item shook Shaun as they went straight to a story of a policeman's body being found in Liverpool with gunshot wounds. He sat motionless as he listened to the story and it appeared that the body he found was an undercover

policeman on the trail of a multimillion pound drug empire and a second body has been found just over half a mile away from the scene of the dead policeman, there are no details given of the 2nd body yet.

"A second body!" he said out loud, he thought, *'Which one did I find? The guy I turned over didn't look like a undercover cop to me, but then again what does a undercover cop look like? My guy had the bag of stuff so maybe was trying to get away and was shot by the cop and the cop may have been shot as well and was wounded and fell to his death with the wounds, though there was no gun by the body I found except in the bag, though I guess he could have dropped it and with all that tall grass and bushes it could have been right next to him and I would never have noticed.*

His mind went from one scenario to the next as he then thought that maybe the guy he found was the policeman and was giving it large on foot to get away, maybe from some meeting that had been jeopardised, *'Shit, am none the wiser, but this sounds really heavy shit to me. A cop down and an unknown body and then me, some bloke with a dog and a big bag of cash who just happened to be walking past, Christ,'* he thought, *'if I was to give the money up now, they might think I had something to do with it as why didn't I come clean earlier and ohh shit am going to be roasted by the police for this and done for perverting the courts of justice etc. and lashed in prison for a long time, God what have I done? Well, one thing for sure, this bag is not going back now.*

The darkness had now fallen and Shaun looked outside for anyone walking by, it was time to get the bag, his house was set off the main road which gave good cover of people looking in the house and both sides of the driveway had large hedges which made it ideal for anyone with a big bag of cash to run back inside the house not noticed. Not taking any chances, he lit up a roll up cig and walked across to the other side of the road to have a great vantage point from all around, *'a few cars went by but the speed they would be going I doubt they would see me,'* he thought, the only thing he was worried about was if there was a neighbourhood peeper. Shaun often sat by the window and was accustomed to have the occasional peep outside himself, which even in this heart pounding moment made him laugh to himself as his favourite comedian told a joke about people who peep and get caught peeping, do you carry on the peep or hide? He looked intensely at all the windows but all the curtains and blinds looked well shut on all the houses around, he pressed the key fob, quickly opened the boot of his car, grabbed the bag with both hands and took the bag inside the house and returned to lock up the car and have another little look around but all was clear.

There was a fair weight inside the bag and Barney was sniffing around the bag one more time, *'well this is it,'* he thought, *'time to open this bag up'*. This time he opened the bag very quickly and started taking out the money and placing it on the table, *'Geez, I didn't realise how heavy money is'*, and as he was grabbing each roll of notes Shaun's eyes kept flickering over to the far side of the holdall towards the gun and after he put all the money on the table he picked up the gun with a dishcloth in case of fingerprints, as the last thing at this moment he needed was his fingerprints on the gun, and placed it on one of the stairs, and then picked up the black box that was in the holdall and placed that with the gun on the stairs in his eagerness to count the money. He opened one roll of money and to his surprise and excitement there was 5 grand! 5 grand to each roll and counting how many rolls there were 50 rolls, *'bloody hell, 250 grand!'* Shaun instantly rolled up another cig and went outside into the garden and sat himself down in the cool air and took in the amount of money he had just counted, repeating the words out loud, "250 grand. 250 grand! Oh yeeeessss."

He finished his cig and went back inside. He picked up the black box, that looked more like some sort of gift box, and opened it. Shaun's eyes opened wide in disbelief as he realised he was looking at a tray of diamonds, "Fucking hell fire!" he exclaimed and stared in amazement. *'These must be worth 10 times the amount of the money I've just found though, what on earth can I do with these?'* His mind was now running at the speed of light trying to work out the best thing to do, but for now he decided to put the diamonds away and so he put the money and the diamonds back in the bag along with the gun, took them upstairs, opened the loft, placed the bag in the loft and closed the hatch.

He went downstairs and just stood there on the spot as he was overwhelmed with it all. He decided to make himself an espresso from the coffee machine he had recently bought from Curry's which he had thought was a steal at £80 as it used to be £160 and on making the coffee he sat down and let the coffee hit the spot. *'I can afford one of them bigger and better coffee machines now but this £80 one certainly did make a good coffee,'* he thought idly. His mind then drifted back to the diamonds and then he remembered quite clearly that a few weeks ago there was a huge jewel heist in London where an alleged 200-million-pound jewel robbery had taken place and putting 2 and 2 together he quickly counted that up to 5 as he was now thinking that this find may be a part of that robbery or somehow connected. The adrenaline had been running at a huge high all day and even the espresso that gave him that extra kick he needed subsided quite quickly as a tiredness like he had never felt before came over him. Barney didn't get his late night walk that night and instead was put out in the garden for a few minutes and Shaun then went straight to bed. As he closed his eyes he hoped he wasn't going to be woken up by a knock on the door with the police waiting.

12th April

Waking up the next day he reached over for his mobile phone to check the time - it was 07:00 and had had probably the best night's sleep he has had since his marriage breakdown over a year ago. He actually felt happy knowing he had a good night's sleep as they was so rare and he headed down the stairs, putting the kettle on and letting Barney into the garden before hitting the bathroom to clean himself up. He was surprised how calm he felt with the whole thing and thought that maybe this is just what he needed to release him from the routine of the last year and the loneliness he has endured. All of a sudden he felt like the old Shaun who was confident and strong minded and his mind focussed on new things rather than wondering what might have been and where it all went wrong.

The thing that made it worse for him was that even though his wife was no good and he hated the way she and her family treated him, he still missed her so strongly at times. One of Shaun's strengths was that he would always try to understand why things weren't working and tried to put things right, but unfortunately his wife and her family were beyond that and the marriage only lasted 2 years but in truth it was over the day he went to live with her and her daughter as they set about destroying it from day 1 and he knew he had bitten off far more than he could chew. He knew that before he married her but somehow hoped he could make a difference, but when something is damaged it stays damaged and like a lot of second marriages its families that cause most of the problems, as its difficult for everyone to get their heads round it for various reasons and if they don't sort it, then failure beckons. He mastered the art of remembering good bits and blanking out all the bad as the pain inside that he had endured those years with her made him so angry with himself for allowing himself to be stupid enough to marry such a woman. But one thing for sure is that he still missed her at times and missed caring for her, maybe it was simply that he just missed caring for her as that itself can sometimes mask as loving someone, but whatever it was he felt let down and betrayed by them and now for the first time in his life he was living alone and, though it takes some getting used to, at least he didn't have to endure the misery of being trapped in a bad marriage. The one thing he did have was his trusty dog Barney and the two of them set out to live their lives on another path once more, and yes there were times when Shaun felt like climbing the walls with anger and despair after 2 failed marriages in his life, though his 1st marriage lasted 20 years and he had 2 daughters and a son who he adored, he didn't think that his next marriage would fail as quickly as 2 years, and starting over again at 54 is not ideal but he also knew that time was a great healer and one day he would banish the memory of his 2 years in a prison with this woman and her daughter. Somehow he needed to find himself again and struggled with it most days and as the months ticked on and the routine he followed as mundane as it was sometimes actually helped him to recover from that ordeal. He often thought about finding another woman but he knew he had to find himself first and wasn't in any hurry to look as sometimes when you search for love all you find is what he found in his latest marriage. He knew that maybe one day he would be out walking his dog and trip over someone's foot and look up and there she will be or maybe not but for now he was OK.

Shaun looked at himself in the mirror whilst shaving and for once he felt good this morning and on seeing his own reflection he smiled at himself and said, "Let's Rock This Joint," which is a favourite saying of his from the film the Mask, he always did like to play the fool and have fun and the people closest to him normally only see that side of him. He would do anything to make people smile and laugh, even at work he was a joker with his colleagues but there was always a serious side of him and he took his job very seriously indeed. The one thing he always said was that with every problem there is always a solution and he loved nothing better than working on the solution rather than giving up something as a bad thing - like when finding the bag he found the right solutions to keep him from being hopefully noticed.

Shaun was back in work the next day and the office was manic at the best of times, though it was funny the way some of his colleagues let off steam when stressed - mostly sarcastic quips shooting across the office, but the bond was very strong between all of them and any differences in his mannerism would be picked up instantly, so he knew he had better be careful tomorrow, not that they would suspect he is 250 grand richer and had a big bag of diamonds, but they would know something was not right.

Walking into the kitchen he hit the switch to the kettle and the first brew of the day was born. Sipping at his tea he switched on the TV for the latest news which would start in 10 minutes, he took his brew out into the garden and, like the first brew, his first roll up cig was created and he sat in the garden and let the nicotine and caffeine do their stuff. Barney was waiting by the gate in the garden, still a bit miffed with not being taken for a walk last night, but as the news was on the TV in a few seconds Shaun took himself in, plonked himself on the sofa and sat there in anticipation of what was about to be said. The news came on and it was dominated by the shootings in Liverpool. Fixed to the spot he listened carefully and, just like what he thought yesterday, this appeared to be connected to the jewel heist in London a few weeks earlier, a picture of the officer who was shot was shown on the TV and he instantly recognised him as the body he had come across on the pathway. His name was Paul Murphy, the other man found dead was London-born Keith Miller who has been associated with underground crime for several years. 5 other men have been arrested and several properties have been raided in London and 2 addresses in Liverpool, Police have yet to comment on the stolen jewels. His thoughts turned to why Liverpool if these guys were from down south. *'Maybe a ship leaving from the port, or maybe these guys are handpicked for a job like this and Liverpool does have its fair share of gangsters, though I guess I would have to be a gangster to fully understand it'*, a thought then came straight to his mind, *'shit, I guess I am a criminal too now by holding on to this money and the diamonds'*. He liked the idea of being a wanted man, and for a few minutes flirted with the idea of being a gangster or maybe a hardened criminal or a fugitive and then laughed and thought *'bloody hell, what am I doing here? But I guess what is done is done, the news tonight should be interesting and hopefully there will be a lot more info then, I just pray that no one saw me leave that path with that bag'*.

Switching off the TV, he decided to take Barney out for a walk but he wasn't going anywhere near the cycle path today and opted for a walk around the estate and small playing fields. His mind was focused on how to spend the cash without suspicion and then he wondered if the cash was old notes and serial numbers that couldn't be traced, *'geez, going to have to check them when I get back in as if they're all random numbers and used notes, then I should be OK, though they didn't look like new notes and if they're not, then happy days'*. As he was strolling the estate his mind drifted towards the money again and he wondered about what a guy does when he is off work with a bundle of cash but just as he entertained the idea he thought against it, *'nope, just wait,'* he thought, *'let's just wait'*.

Due to moving away from the area for a few years he didn't have too many friends, and what friends he did have were simply too busy in their own lives but he knew he could call on them if he wanted. But with the hurt of his marriage breakdown all he wanted to do was hide and get his own shit together before breaking out into this sometimes cruel world, however he did keep in constant touch with his own kids from his first marriage and loved his kids immensely and would share laughs and good advice on the phone to them and occasionally go to see them which was always great but he knew also that he didn't see them enough but again this was due to him shutting down after his marriage breakdown. He thought that maybe, in time, when he has recovered from all of this crap and the feeling of wanting to barricade the doors when he gets home eases, he may once again be himself as he felt let down by the world and needed to lick his wounds for a while longer.

He set about the rest of the day doing the one thing he loved and that was pottering about the garden. As a kid growing up in the streets of Anfield he never had a garden and all of the houses had had back yards so why he loved it he would never know, maybe even as a small child he dreamed of a better place to be with all the trimmings. What started out a few years ago with buying a few plants and some pots has now turned into some sort of obsession but an obsession that he can see so much beauty in. The thought of planting some seeds and watching them grow and caring for them kind of kept him in touch with nature and he did have a very caring nature himself, even at times going to great lengths to save bees that had fallen into the pond when he lived with his ex-wife. He was always a thinker and the urge to understand science and nature was always the motivation with Shaun and he longed for a better understanding of the universe, he thought that maybe now he could buy that high-powered telescope he has always wanted.

Though his own nature was calm and understanding he did have one hell of a temper which, when it came out, was hard to stop. This side was very rare and took something like betraying his trust or hurting his family before it would come out and then all hell on earth would be unleashed from his mouth, but as soon as he got it all out he would quickly calm down and, as he didn't like holding a grudge, he would try to sort it out properly with reason.

Gardening was a good fit for him as it kept his ever-thinking mind occupied and he got something special out of it and a sense of achievement. Today though as he tendered his garden his thoughts were only on the money and he had been in the garden for nearly 3 hours and had got some good jobs done out there, but more importantly his plans for the money were now starting to seed too and he went over all his actions from yesterday step by step. In his younger days he played guitar in a punk band and loved the thrill of performing on stage and, like his gambling he loved the kick of that too, he was always at his best on stage and delivering some new songs he had written, always creative and looking for the buzz of playing, yet there was a totally different side of him too. The performing lunatic on stage and the gentleman off stage, *'a Dr Jekyll and Mr Hyde so to speak, I guess everyone has a side that they would like to come out,'* and he did it with some success along the way too.

Right here and now though he was 54 years old and the days of excitement and mayhem are gone but not forgotten and even though the last year had been so hard for him he still had hopes of doing a few more exciting things; such as a trip to Vegas as that has always been a thing he wanted to do and do it large and make sure what happens in Vegas stays in Vegas too, though he was single now and so he reasoned he could tell his friends at work how he gambled and drank and fucked his way through Vegas and came back for more as after all that's what Vegas is there for! He came back inside the house for the 1 o'clock news and, again, the story was making all the headlines but the main headline was that huge amounts of high valued goods have been seized from properties in and around the London area and 7 arrests have now been made, as for the shootings in Liverpool, the police feel that it may be connected to this but are keeping an open mind on it, the police also say some of the goods may have already left the country and they are confident of further arrests. *'Bloody hell, they seem like amateurs, why would they split all the goods up and keep them in their houses? Surely they would have had buyers for them or were working for someone big and they have had a huge pay day as a result, or maybe the main jewels have been taken and all the other stuff left with them to sort of throw people off the scent. I can understand cash being split up but diamonds and jewellery you have to have a market for it, though what I do know, but what I do know is that I have 150 sparkling pieces in my loft and they're a good size, especially 3 of them, News at 10 should be good tonight.'*

Cups of tea and sandwiches were what he ate most of when he was at home as it was an easy fix, but he always tried to make some sort of cooked meal for his evening meal but, for now, he broke out the bread and threw some ham on it and made another brew and enjoyed his butties.

After he had eaten all his sandwiches he decided to get out the house for a while and jumped into his car. He thought he would take a drive past the scene of the 2 found bodies, there were 2 entrances to the path that he used and the body of the cop was right in between them so there had to be activity around these entrances he figured. He took a right turn towards the 1st entrance off Muirhead avenue and as he did he noticed 2 big white vans and 3 police cars parked alongside the road. He drove straight past them, slowed down to take a sharp left turn and, quickly glancing over, he could see police in uniform and some in plain clothes gathered together talking. *'Looks like all the brains are hard at work now,'* he thought as he took a right turn to head towards the second entrance on Broadway, he could now feel the excitement returning to him and a strong feeling of being in control. As he approached the 2nd entrance he could see that this path had been taped up and no one was allowed though. Pulling up the car next to one of the local shops he thought he would buy a paper and try to listen to any local gossip.

He walked into the shop and picked up the Liverpool Echo newspaper and its headlines were all about the shootings and arrests, he walked over to the shop assistant and said "Police everywhere around here today, what's happened?"

"Don't you read the papers mate or watch the news?" replied the shop keeper, "it's been like gun fight at the O.K. Corral around here!"

Trying to look surprised Shaun replied, "Oh yeah, I heard about that but I didn't know it was around here."

"Yeah, madness," said the shop keeper, "but business is good for me, keeping all the police officers with fresh sandwiches and coffee all day," he joked.

Shaun laughed, "Yeah, I bet you get to hear all the latest news before everyone else!"

The shop keeper couldn't help but reel off what he had heard from the police, "They got some house cordoned off just around the corner from here."

"Wow, local gangsters eh!"

"Yeah he is and often comes into my shop, though never smiles or talks to me, he just asks for his cigs and that's it, he is a big guy, not one to mess with, they call him Ajay."

Shaun replied, "I think the police will be smoking his cigs today," and laughed.

The shop keeper then came out with something really interesting for Shaun when he said, "I just hope they don't find what they're looking for as I am making a fortune selling my sandwiches to them throughout the day and night, looking for it!"

"Is there another body or something?" Shaun asked.

"Am not sure," said the shop keeper, "all I know is that I heard a copper say if it's not there, then it must be in the house."

"Oh well," said Shaun, "let's hope they don't find it for a while then, eh?" he added as he walked out the shop.

Getting into his car he glanced over at the pathway and at the police and thought *'if only they knew'* and smiled to himself. He lit up a roll up and, on driving away, he knew the police was most probably looking for the bag and he played back the shop keeper's words in his mind that whatever they are looking for may be in the house! *'Yes, my house'*.

On getting home he took out the paper he bought and started to read it, the bloke called Ajay was not mentioned in it but the house cordoned off around the corner was, *'7 arrests, likely to be 8 soon I think'*. Interestingly though as he read through the article he saw that the 7 arrests in London are known professional gangsters and not amateurs like he had thought and further arrests were likely, *'I guess with a 200-million-pound robbery the police are going to have to arrest the whole bloody lot'*. Sitting on the sofa he then started to look at it more realistically, *'the bank want their diamonds back, the people who they belonged to want them back, the police want them back and the gangsters want them back too so I think all of them will stop at nothing to get them back, even my 150 pieces of sparkling gems and the money'.*

His mind was going deeper into it and he didn't fancy sleeping with the fishes if he got caught or being locked up in a prison somewhere or even running scared for most of his life, but he had to get something from this. *'The money is never going back, but the diamonds may have to unless I keep them and make them my little secret till the day I die, but if I did give them back to the police, sooner rather than later, my name would get out and I would be become another mistaken identity drive by shooting victim! The bank would love them back but they would hand me over to the police and again boom! Dead! And as for knocking on Ajay's door and saying "Hi, are these your diamonds?" I would probably never be found again, though it looks like he will be going down for a good while if he has anything to do with them shootings or diamonds. I guess the only thing I can do is nothing and just keep sitting back and see how the show unfolds',* which would be difficult for him as he normally likes to jump straight in head first, but this time he knows he has to keep calm as maybe his life depends on it!

He got busy getting his clothes ready for work for the next day, ironing was something he hated with a passion, he could tidy up all day and even loved shopping but the ironing he detested and it made him so angry, why it made him so angry he would never know, yet his ex-wife could iron all day and night and enjoyed it, she loved nothing better than ironing which he always thought was weird, but he had always seen ironing as a time consuming pain in the arse, though he could iron a shirt better than his ex as she always messed up the collar. After 5 shirts, one for each day, and 2 pairs of trousers he called the ironing a day, he had often thought of getting his laundry washed and ironed for him by the woman in the laundrette or asking maybe someone local to do it but, until now, money was tight but that may change now.

Another good thing he thought of was that in the last 24 hours he has hardly thought of his ex-wife and felt the loneliness, as in the early part of their split it would drive him crazy thinking about her, and even in the last few months he wished he could stop thinking about her at times but when you live on your own you tend to move more slowly in your mind as you have that much time to think of things due to all the excess time on your hands and even though it was over a year, at times it felt as fresh as ever. He often thought about meeting someone else, just to make himself stop thinking about her and his present situation, but that wasn't the right thing to do as he needed to let go of the sadness in him first and it wasn't fair for the woman he would meet as well, sometimes the sadness after a while becomes the only friend you have and he knew this was dangerous and he had to let go for his own health as he was aware he may be heading for depression and that is so difficult to shake off judging by how one of his best friends struggled with depression.

He tried several hobbies to keep his mind focused but nothing except for his gardening did it for him, he had his PC which he often spent hours sitting over either watching music on YouTube or playing his favourite fantasy football, in fact he used to be an avid gamer for many years on the PC and consoles but didn't seem to have the same enthusiasm for that now. Looking back at his younger years he would sit up all night on the PC playing Football Manager and the sleep he lost with that over the years was madness but he had always kept on going to make sure he managed Liverpool FC and take them to glory.

Having split up with his wife and for all the right reasons it still doesn't prepare you for going it alone. Some people jump straight into another relationship but most of the time they're only kidding themselves with that, and even though hobbies weren't working for him he wasn't ready for a new relationship in the first 6 months afterwards, and then the next 3 months he was kind of flirting with the idea of it and it's only now, 13 months down the line, he feels that maybe, just maybe, he may be ready as in the last few months he hasn't looked back as much as he did and has been making more plans for the future and slowly starting to get the feeling of being alive again. He knew he was getting there but just wished he could get there a little quicker and the problem is when you're a deep thinker you tend to stay messed up and in thoughts a lot longer but maybe this money and the diamonds may be the kick-start he has been looking for.

He walked over to get his jacket and took Barney out for a walk, walking was never a great hobby of his but he knew it did him good as well as Barney and it's amazing how many people you meet by simply walking your dog. His mind was a lot clearer now that all the adrenaline had gone and he could feel the change even within 24 hours within himself as he felt so much more positive and stronger, maybe it was the acceptance of his new-found wealth and the idea of changing the things he wanted to change. He took his time to say hello to a woman walking her own dog.

She instantly said, "Wasn't that awful them 2 shootings on the bike path?" and she went into great detail about how many times a week she walks her dog on that path.

"Yeah, I walk my dog there too," he said, but before he could say anything else she went off on one, as if she had all the answers for everything, saying she doesn't feel safe walking there now.

Shaun told her that the 2 dead guys probably weren't walking dogs there now and so she should be OK. She laughed and said, "I guess so, but it's still a scary thought."

He could see her point and, pulling Barney away, he thought, *'it seems everyone is talking about it so I guess I better do the same as I am going to look the odd one out otherwise'*.

As he walked the estate his mind then went back to the diamonds he had, he knew as long as he was careful with the money he would be OK and have a good life but the diamonds were a sticking point and he knew that he couldn't rest knowing that they were there as too many times in the last 24 hours they kept on coming back to him. *'I wonder if the cash was from the raid too or was that some sort of payment for them, maybe the undercover cop had set up a meeting and it all went wrong and made a run for it with the diamonds and the money and got shot as a result or maybe the cop had other intentions and was trying to make a fortune for himself or simply just an unlucky guy who fucked up in the night?'* He asked himself questions like this as he had to know, it was always like this for Shaun, wanting to know why and what and when and where and who as he had such an inquisitive mind.

As he waited to cross the road a new Land Rover went passed, *'now that's a car,'* he thought, *'maybe that's the first thing I buy when the dust has settled, though not a new one but maybe a second hand one that looks new'*. He loved his cars and drove a very sporty looking Toyota Celica, it was, however, getting old now but could still certainly shift, his friend had had a Land Rover many years ago and he had loved having a drive of that and the new models looked awesome. The reality of whatever he wanted was sinking in now, *'a car, my own place, a holiday, but am going to have to look at how to spend money without raising questions from others, geez this is going to be difficult'*.

He thought about setting up a little fake business and paying money into the bank every few weeks but what type of business? *'Maybe a gardening business, though am sure it cannot be that easy to do'*, then the thought of work came into his mind, he could take early retirement and live quite comfortable for the rest of his years rather than flog himself to death, but then he loved his job and would miss all the people he works with and the opportunities that come his way, *'no, think that idea is out of the question but it's something to think about a bit more as there may be voluntary redundancies coming in at the end of the year'*.

He got back to his house, looked in the fridge and realised that if he wanted to eat any more today, he had better go to the shops, to break the monotony of doing the same things he would often switch supermarkets by going to Sainsbury's one week, the next Tesco, and the next Asda. and preferred to do the shopping of an evening around 9pm as the stores didn't have too many people in them and he didn't have to dodge all the irresponsible trolley drivers and the mothers with all the screaming kids, at night it was much more relaxed, though the Tiger bread was always gone and if any was left, it was more like Tiger Brick as it had gone as hard as rock.

The main advantage of going in the evening was that there were more bargains in the 'whoops' aisles with 50% off and, in some cases, 90% off its advertised price as it had to be eaten that day. He had lost count of how many midnight feasts he had had in the last year courtesy of the 'whoops' aisle. He had to go a little earlier tonight as he had to get back to see News at 10, so he decided to go at 7pm and until then he just potted around the garden some more.

One thing he liked to do when shopping was to be on the lookout for a potential new woman friend as you do tend to get a lot of single woman doing shopping late at night and probably, like him, do their shopping late to break up the boredom of sitting in the house by breaking up their day. He had a terrible habit that he couldn't kick and it all stemmed from the years he had played in his rock band - any woman that he sees he scores out of 10 and he had spent many evenings with his band mates debating like crazy how on earth she was a 7 or an 8 and now and again a 9 but no one ever agreed if someone said there was a 10. Yes, as childish as it was, it was great fun at the time but it simply stuck with him and he would be walking around Asda and in his mind saying *'6...that's a 5... oh, 2... hmm, 7...'* But all these years later and being 54 means that a score of 10 has a total new meaning and his son often joked with him saying, "Dad, at your age, do you give them 2 points for just breathing?" which always made him laugh.

Yes, he knew it was the heart and soul that mattered but there must be an attraction, well, at least with Shaun there had to be. Going around the bread aisle he noticed a few 3s, followed by a zero which scared the hell out of him and he left the scene fast, and as he picked up some frozen fish he noticed a 6 mm, *'not bad,'* he thought but the thought quickly faded when her husband appeared on the scene. After picking up some essentials such as a huge Toblerone and more Wiltshire ham he opted for the checkout and looked over at the tills for his favourite assistant as she always made a big fuss of him and he liked that, the assistant was originally from India and had a great outlook on life. She was so happy in herself and over the last year he had had many chats with her and often thought about what a great lady she is, the last time he spoke to her she went on at great length about how to cook a joint of beef he bought and he followed her advice when he cooked it and he was so glad he took her advice as it tasted delicious.

On getting home he put the fish in the oven, wrapped up in tin foil with a little water inside, placed the veg in the pans and destroyed the meal by making some instant mash, but he loved it.

Whilst he was preparing his tea he felt pretty good about himself and in control of his own destiny and enjoying life once more. When his meal was ready to eat he sat there with some bread rolls and got stuck in. As he was eating his mind drifted back to the diamonds and let the permutations of what he could do with them entertain his mind and, before he knew it, his meal was eaten. He took the plates out straight away and cleaned them as he hated nothing more than seeing a sink full of dirty plates and knew it made sense to keep on top of the cleaning etc. His back kitchen would always have to be nice, the rest of the house could be a mess but not the kitchen or the back kitchen as they say in Liverpool.

He made himself a drink and plonked himself down on the PC and looked for the latest information on the bank heist and the shooting in Liverpool. He clicked around from site to site wondering if all the people accessing these sites could be traced but he dismissed it as who would monitor news channels as there would be thousands of people accessing them and, as it stands, the police are well on top of the situation. The more he read, the more uncomfortable he became, and from feeling strong an hour ago he was now feeling anxious and, in truth, a little scared.

Later that night he switched on the TV and sat on the sofa with a brew and waited for News at 10. It's headlines were that there had been a further arrest in Liverpool over the shootings, it was the man whose house was cordoned off in Liverpool. When they went over to the scene the journalist gave a full description of the man arrested and said a fair amount of items have been found in the house, and police say an eyewitness who had seen 3 men running towards the cycle path just before the shootings happened has been giving the police details of the men and the police have been going door to door in the neighbourhood asking residents if they heard or saw anything suspicious that evening. *'Shit.'* thought Shaun, *'I hope they don't knock on the man's house who was fixing his garage roof!'*

"Shit! Shit!" he shouted loudly.

'Did he see me throw the bag in the car?' He cast his mind back over the point that he noticed the man on top of the garage and he appeared to be looking away from him rather than at him but maybe he turned around! The story then went over to London for more information on the heist

and more arrests have been made there and they believe that at least half of the items that were stolen from the vault have now been recovered. The story then moved to the dead policeman in Liverpool, saying that his funeral is to be held sometime next week, but still no details of why the policeman, Paul Murphy, was there that night. Switching off the TV he put his coat on and took Barney out for a walk around the estate.

His mind was racing with thoughts and on his return to the house he went into the garden, sat on the bench, lit a cig and tried to make sense of what he had heard on the news. *'Why was the cop there and why won't the police say?'* Putting his cig out he came back inside, locked everywhere up and went to bed. He lay in bed thinking about why he took the bag and ran as, if he did get caught, he would more than likely be sacked from his good job and maybe even put in prison and all the values he has tried to teach his own children growing up would be worthless. He felt anxious and tossed and turned as the possibility he had been seen by the man on the garage roof became a nightmare, he could still see the body in the tall grass in his mind and eventually fell asleep exhausted with it all.

13th April

The next morning, he looked at the time and, like so many mornings, he had woken up 2 minutes before the alarm went off. He quickly cancelled the alarm as he didn't want it to go off as he hated the sound of it, maybe that's what woke him up as his brain didn't want to hear that sound. Walking into the bathroom he caught a glimpse of himself in the mirror and thought, *'geez, I look rough today,'* the tossing and turning of his night's sleep had caught up with him. He walked down the stairs to be greeted by Barney and, after making a fuss of him, he put the kettle on and made a brew. The morning ritual seemed slightly different today for some reason as he fed the birds and lit up the 1st roll up of the day and drank his tea. Barney was waiting at the gate looking over at him as he knows once that cig is finished he would be going for a walk. He clipped the lead on his collar and headed off for a walk with Barney and even though he felt tired from his restless sleep his mind was now wide awake and thinking more about the whole situation.

When he got back from the walk he took the 3 S's S--t shower and shave and followed this by putting his suit for work. He always left the TV on for the dog and gave him a rawhide strip and then jumped into his car and went to work.

Normally his car radio was set for Talk Sport but today he changed channels to get the best news updates on the robbery and shootings, he knew when he got to work he had to act normal and try to keep focused on his job, though there was not much more news on the radio so he switched it off and pulled up at the Tesco garage for some fuel. He got a coffee from the Costa vending machine which, surprisingly, tasted pretty good for a vending machine. The coffee was hitting the spot as he worked through the morning traffic to get to work and on reaching the NCP car park in the town centre he parked up and headed into work. He felt a growing confidence as he walked into the work place and was greeted with the usual tones of "Morning" which was never really said with any enthusiasm.

"Yeah, morning all," he replied and headed straight for the kettle to brew up.

His job was a busy job and he always tried his best and also tried to hide the real him as he didn't really want his colleagues to know he was struggling at times with the breakdown of his marriage.

After about 2 hours the Office Team Organiser said, "You seem full of yourself today, did you have a good breakfast or has some evil woman had their wicked way with you last night, as you seem really efficient today and bouncing!"

"Oh right, err, do I," he instantly came up with a little white lie as he said, "ohh, I just had a good night's sleep that's all, nothing exciting like that happened. But if you know any evil women, then send them over to me!"

'You can never hide anything from a woman they say and with Katie that was a fact however I think she bought my reply,' he thought.

Later on that day it was inevitable that someone in the office was going to mention the shootings around his way and sure enough it came, "Hey, Shaun, what's with all the shootings by where you live?! We heard they was shooting at you with all the bad jokes you tell!"

"Ha-ha, yeah right," replied Shaun, and then said, "they couldn't hit me I am far too quick for them to shoot at and anyways you always laugh at my jokes! They reckon it may be part of that jewel heist or something, crazy times, eh?"

Andy wasn't from Liverpool so his next reply was expected as well, "You're all nutters and robbers from Liverpool and by the time you Scousers have finished shooting there will be no Scousers left to shoot!"

Shaun quickly replied, "Dream on mate, and watch you don't choke on your pie, you pie eating git," to which they both laughed and carried on with their day.

5pm soon came along and Shaun jumped into his car, powered up the engine, hit the radio button and set off home, the news did highlight the robbery but it appeared now that maybe other things were taking the headlines. He pulled up at one of the local shops and bought the Liverpool Echo and The Times, he wouldn't normally buy The Times but he wanted to get a wider view of what is going on with the robbery and, with it being a Southern type of paper, he thought it may go a bit deeper into the story.

As he got home the opening of the door ritual started as he walked into the house with Barney bringing a scruffy toy in his mouth to him but, as always, he wouldn't let go of it if you tried to take it off him and once the greeting was over he would wait patiently by the door waiting to go out for a walk. He grabbed the lead and took Barney out.

The day had passed quickly but he was aware that he was only going through the motions at work and his mind was elsewhere, he greeted other dog walkers he met and when he got to the playing field he let Barney off the lead. He sat on a small wall and thoughts of his ex-wife and his old life filled his mind and, even though he knew it was stupid to do it, he still opened up a picture of her on his mobile phone. Looking deep into the picture he thought to himself, *'the stupid bitch,'* but he still gave a small smile and looked up to the sky and said to himself, "It's murder letting go but I have to, it's for the best."

After a while he took Barney home and set about making a bite to eat and, after carefully looking in the freezer, he decided on fish and butter sauce with some chips and, as always, some bread and butter. Whilst his meal was cooking he grabbed a quick shower and a change of clothes, fed Barney, and then sat down to eat his fish and butter sauce tea.

He flicked on the TV for the latest news and, whilst waiting for the news, he started to read through the newspapers whilst throwing his meal into his mouth at a fast rate as he was starving. He noticed a large piece on the robbery and read it right through, *'bloody hell, nothing I already don't know… and same with the local newspaper'.* He threw the papers to one side and waited for the news on the TV and finished off his tea. When the news came on he sat there not expecting much but sat there open-mouthed when the main story was that there were 9 men arrested and held in custody and large amounts of high value goods have now been retrieved at several locations. Police have detained others at these locations, They believe that about 80% of the goods stolen have now been retrieved and are confident of finding further items. The men arrested had their faces shown on TV and some video footage of them in the vault carrying out the robbery with the newsman stating that further reports will be available on the 9 o'clock news this evening.

Shaun sat there shaking his head, *'geez, what a catch that was by the police,'* he thought, *'I wonder how they pieced all that together, someone must have messed up huge in the gang or someone let something slip, or simply tried to spend some of the money or maybe sell some of the jewels. Well, I ain't going to start spending just yet or speak to no one about anything, and as for the diamonds well, they can just wait until I know what to do with them'.*

9 o'clock soon came around and the whole story came out and even further high value goods have been retrieved and in total 12 arrests have been made, police now think at least 90% of all items have been recovered from the robbery. The police stated that they have been working tirelessly over the last few weeks and have had several people watched and only pounced when they had enough evidence and intelligence to arrest all involved. "The man shot in Liverpool was not connected to the robbery. However, we believe he was involved in trying to organise the movement of large quantities of the stolen items and the undercover policeman was shot in the process of trying to gather evidence."

Shaun said to himself, "Hang on, if he shot the policeman, then who shot the gangster?"

He sat there trying to work it out, *'maybe they policeman shot him 1st and got shot himself and as he ran away he died of his wounds or maybe he was hiding from someone else in the tall grass on the embankment and died of his wounds and the others couldn't find him as it's pitch black on that cycle track of a night with all the trees and high embankments and no lighting. Thinking it over again, the man arrested in Liverpool by the name of Ajay has probably explained to the police why he was involved. And the man was shot trying to retrieve a bag of cash and some diamonds and if he has told all, then the police will certainly be looking for the Bag! As, if he didn't have it, then who did?!'*

Another brew was needed as he started to feel anxious as it appeared that, one by one, everyone from the heist to the shootings was now arrested and the full story was coming out. As he sipped his tea he went over his steps again and that bloody man on the garage roof crossed his mind again. Then he thought maybe a cyclist went past as they were so fast that he wouldn't have noticed them passing while he was staring at the body of the policeman, though they would have come forward by now, *'or maybe they have and they're still looking for that someone with the bag! Though the likelihood of them seeing me up the embankment was slim and even then, they would have just thought it was a bloke out walking his dog maybe'*… "Geez, what the hell have I done?" he asked himself in a low voice.

An hour had soon passed and now News at 10 was giving even more details about the London-based gang and it appears that they were well established criminals and professionals at what they did. And they were linked to many robberies over many years and this was meant to be the last big job they did. So they got everyone they knew together, carried out the job, split up all the money and jewels, and went their separate ways. *'Which probably explains why they didn't all have buyers for the jewels and stuff just yet,'* Shaun reasoned. *'Plan A worked and, more than likely, Plan B didn't get going, but either way it was a very bold job they did.'* The newsreader read it out like he was telling a Hollywood movie by saying old time robbers were trying out their skills one last time in pulling off a near perfect crime, only to be foiled by perfect police work.

Switching off the TV he clipped the lead on Barney and headed for an evening walk around the estate. He still felt anxious and his mind was racing, though the walk did help somewhat and on his return home he locked up and went to bed, thinking of all sorts of scenarios, and eventually fell asleep exhausted.

14th April

Reaching over to his phone to shut his alarm off as usual before it went off he sluggishly got out of bed. *'Shit, am worn out with all this worry,'* he thought as he made his way to the bathroom. He splashed cold water on his face, he could feel the refreshing value of it as he did it one more time before heading off downstairs to make a brew and the morning ritual of making a big fuss of Barney. As he stepped into the garden and sipped on his tea he somehow felt edgy this morning, something just didn't feel quite right. Ever since Shaun was a young boy he had had these sort of feelings and it was always like a warning or prelude to something. As a result, he trusted these feelings as they have served him well in the past, though for the life of him he couldn't understand why he got these feelings. Was he being looked after by some celestial being or was it simply being in touch with his brain and senses or, as his mum used to say to him when he was a young lad, that he was given a gift by her mum, whatever the reason, he trusted these feelings and always kept a careful eye on things.

From being sluggish his brain started to come alive and he could now think clearer. He fed the birds as usual and as he was filling the bird feeders the birds gathered in the hedges, waiting for their morning feast of seed and mealworm. He made the first roll up of the day and sat there and enjoyed the moment of caffeine and nicotine and watched the birds fill their faces. Tea and cig finished, he then took Barney out for his morning walk.

It was a very cold morning and he wished he had put a hat on as the cold wind hurt his ears, making him feel uncomfortable, *'maybe am coming down with something as I don't feel right at all'*.

On getting back home he proceeded to the bathroom for the 3 S's. Whilst in the shower, the hot water beating against his body felt more soothing than most days, *'is it because I am cold,'* he thought, *'or simply the whole thing of the money and the diamonds and not forgetting the gun is catching up on me?'* As he got out the shower, dried himself and then started to shave he realised he still felt anxious, *'fuck, something's not right here'*.

After getting ready he jumped into the car and headed off to work. He stopped off at the Tesco garage to grab a coffee and a croissant. Throwing the croissant down his neck along with the coffee whilst he drove through the mad traffic this morning made him feel a little easier with things, except for the mess the croissant was making. He pulled up in the car park and lit up a cig. He knew that he couldn't carry on with his work whilst he was like this and sat there, thinking of excuses to make to have the rest of the week off work. The 3 C's were now doing the trick: caffeine croissant and cig and the plan was born. *'Oh, for the routine of the 3 S's and 3 C's,'* he thought every day.

As he walked into the office he said his good mornings. He looked at his planner for the rest of the week and said to Katie, his team organiser, "Am going to take the rest of the week off from tomorrow as I haven't been sleeping too well of late and I feel run down. So, as my planner is free, am going to take these days off and try to get back to my best."

Katie replied, "You haven't had time off in ages and that's what is probably wrong with you, you should have had the whole week off Shaun."

"Yeah, maybe. But I had some loose ends to tie up today and I should be good for some time off then."

Katie offered him some paracetamol, "Yeah, give us 2 of them please Katie as I got a bit of a temperature."

"Man flu, is it?" she said sarcastically.

"Yeah, it's tough being a bloke," he replied.

"Ha, yeah right," Katie said, "You wouldn't last 5 minutes as a woman."

Katie was a lot younger than Shaun but she had a very old head on her shoulders and he always confided in her when things weren't too good. In fact, he treated her just like one of his own daughters rather than his team organiser and he also knew how difficult it was running a house with all the bills etc. But to be a single parent like her, with a 6-year-old daughter, and trying to balance work and bills and home life must be so much more difficult and he admired her for her strengths, and even got strength from her just by talking to her. Swallowing the paracetamol and switching on the laptop, he tried to get through the many emails that awaited him.

"You sure you're OK, Shaun?" she asked again.

"Yeah, will have a chat with you later Katie."

"OK," she replied, "well, put the kettle on Shaun and, err, while you're there throw some bread in the toaster for me!"

"Hey, am supposed to be sick," he laughed, as she had him running around after her all the time and, as always, he did what he was told and put the kettle on and made her toast.

It was at this point when some other people's heads popped up from behind their desks and said, "Hey, you brewing up? Good lad, mine's a coffee."

"Tea for me!" shouted Andy.

"Bloody hell guys, am feeling like crap today, you should be making my brew!"

A barrage of friendly sarcasm came from all sides of the office and the 1st office brew of the day was born. As soon as they all had their drinks the office descended back into that weird kind of silence, except for that annoying sound of the printer which seemed to be non-stop all day.

He had a meeting at 10:30 and got all his paperwork ready for it, though for a few moments the money and the diamonds and the body started to drift back into his mind, *'geez, concentrate,'* he thought to himself. He started to discuss part of the meeting's agenda with his colleagues. Being focused on his job really helped him cope with all the stress of learning to live on his own again and deal with the nasty aftermath of separation from his wife and he could use his work to put it all behind him, but today the pressure and that anxious feeling was starting to get a bit too much for him and he headed into the meeting not as confidently as he would like. *'Now's the time to throw a few seeds down,'* he thought as he opened up by saying he

48

was going to keep it short today as he wasn't feeling too good, it appeared most people were happy with that.

The meeting went well and he finished off his day as quickly as he could, all the guys in the office were telling him how to get better quickly with all their fantastic remedies such as a Beechams' hot lemon drink and then a hot bath and the famous 'have a whiskey in your tea', a hot toddy before you go to bed. They all bought the fact he wasn't well as he clearly wasn't himself so they had no reason to question it. Shaun left the office and headed to the car park via Costa Coffee and bought himself a large latte. Sitting in the car he gathered up his thoughts. He decided to take a drive by the scene and call in at the local shop and talk to his chatty assistant.

When he got there, there was still a police car by the entrance but that was it. Stepping out of the car he walked into the shop and started to look around some of the aisles, as if he was looking for something particular, to draw conversation from the man.

"Where is your dog food mate?"

The man just pointed to the bottom right aisle, "Cheers mate," he said as he picked up a few tins of dog food and went over to the counter, "oh, can I have the Liverpool Echo please and 25 gram Golden Virginia."

As the man reached over for the tobacco Shaun then jumped in with, "It's a lot quieter here today than the other day I was in here, you couldn't move for bloody policeman."

"Yeah," said the assistant, "they have packed up all the gear now and most have gone, seems they have it all done."

Shaun quickly jumped in again by saying, "You was doing well selling all them sandwiches to them."

"Yes," laughed the man, "for 3 days I made a killing but today am left with a load of sandwiches that I doubt I will sell."

Shaun looked at the man and smiled and said, "Well, I tell you what, I will buy one of the BLT sandwiches as am starving."

The man smiled back and then Shaun delivered the next question, "The other day you said the police was looking for something, did they manage to find it?"

"Am not sure," the man replied, "but I tell you what, if you would have dropped a 10 pence piece in the tall grass they would have found it as they turned over every blade of grass for at least 1 mile!"

Shaun laughed and said, "I dropped a cigarette lighter on that path about a year ago, I wonder if they found that!"

The man laughed too and Shaun left the shop.

As he got in the car he felt he needed to take a walk along the path once more, maybe just out of curiosity or simply he had to for his own peace of mind. He drove home, grabbed the lead, put Barney in the car and headed for the entrance where he had parked his car on the day of the find. Barney was pulling at the lead with excitement when he took him out of the car and headed for the path. There was no police presence here and after looking up the path and seeing no one else in sight he let Barney off the lead. Straight away, Barney headed up the embankment and tall grass and chased every bird in sight along the way, as he drew closer to the spot he found the bag and the body he could feel the anxiousness returning and he called

Barney back to him. As Barney came running back down the embankment he suddenly stopped and stared at the trees.

"Hello!" said a voice behind him and Shaun nearly froze on the spot as he turned around to see 2 policemen standing next to a tree high in the embankment, right by where the body had been lying.

"A'right lads, what's up?" Shaun asked.

"Can you wait there a minute mate whilst we come down as we would like to ask you a few questions."

"Yeah, sure, OK," he replied.

Shaun's heart was now beating very quickly and he thought that it was not a good idea coming here and as the police drew closer his heart was banging in his chest, *'geez man, calm yourself,'* he thought.

He shouted for Barney to come over and put the lead back on him as the police came next to him. Barney was making a big fuss of the policemen and one of the policemen stroked him and made a fuss back, but one was a narky looking git and wasn't interested in the dog at all.

"Friendly dog, isn't it mate?"

"Yeah, loves people and kids, but can be funny with other dogs though."

"Yeah, Jack Russell's can be like that," said the friendly copper, "just a few questions, if you don't mind. Do you walk your dog often up this path?"

"Err, more now and again really, sometimes once a week and then maybe leave it for a few weeks before I come back as I tend to split my walking up between here and Croxteth Park and just around my own estate, in fact, mainly 'round my own estate."

The next question Shaun knew was coming, "So when was the last time you came here?"

"Err, last weekend, err, Saturday, it was in the afternoon."

"What time in the afternoon?" asked the miserable policeman.

"Err, about 3 o'clock, maybe half 3."

"Where exactly did you walk from and to?"

"Same as I always do really - I start off at the West Derby entrance and walk to the Broadway entrance and then head back as what am doing now."

"Did you notice anything out of the ordinary?"

"No, not really, though there seemed more cyclists than normal that day as I was forever keeping hold of my dog to let them past."

"Did you notice any other people or dog walkers?"

"Err, come to think of it, I remember a family walking down the path, there was a young woman and man with a couple of kids pushing a pram and, as my dog loves kids, he ran over to them and they was stroking him, but that's about it really."

"Did you notice anyone on the higher ground of the embankment where we just come from?"

"No, I cannot remember anything like that, though plenty of people do tend to walk their dogs up there, even I used to when the dog was a bit younger and I was a bit younger too, but I tend to stay low level now," Shaun then came straight out with it, "is this to do with the shootings?"

"Yes," they both said.

"Crazy times, eh lads?" Shaun answered back.

The police then gave him a card with a special number on it and told him that if he thinks of anything later, that may be useful to them, then to call that number.

"Will do lads, goodnight."

Shaun walked away from the 2 policeman and his legs felt like jelly but he kept on walking and didn't turn round, *'phew, that was crazy,'* he thought and as he reached the other entrance he decided to have a cig and calm himself down a bit before heading back down the path. As he got close to where the 2 policeman came out from there was no sign of them anywhere and he tried to act as calmly as he could, took the ball out of his coat pocket and started to throw it down the path for Barney to run after. He walked slightly faster to get back to the other entrance, and as he reached the entrance he looked down the path but no one was in sight. Opening the car door for Barney to jump in he quickly got in himself and drove home. He had half expected the police to still be there and, strangely enough, he kind of enjoyed the experience of it, the feeling of being scared yet in control gave him an excitement that he had seldom had before, it was like he needed to speak to the police and also needed to walk past the crime scene.

He sat on the sofa and looked at the hotline number card the police had given him and smiled as he knew they hadn't a clue about him, that was cause for a celebration. He made a brew, fed Barney, took his tea outside and ate the BLT butty he had got from the shop. After he devoured the butty he had a cig as all the anxiousness of the day had now passed and all that remained was a sense of well-being and a kind of natural high. He sat there thinking of his find and the diamonds and wished it was only the money he found but couldn't bear to give the diamonds back or maybe even throw them away. Reflecting on the talk with the police it was obvious they were still looking for clues on the shootings and possibly looking for clues on the whereabouts of the bag.

That night he scoured away through all the reports of the robbery and how the figure of 200 million may have been stolen, in some reports it was 10 million plus. He learnt how the gang got into the vault and made their getaway, maybe it was watching all them old time gangster movies with his father as a child that meant he had some sort of admiration for the gangsters for what nearly turned out to be the perfect crime. Reading one article it stated that it may have been set up by someone inside the bank or maybe an insurance job, *'hmm, a win-win situation,'* he thought. The thing is, now he had gone too far with this and he knew that he couldn't give the diamonds back to them, *'well, maybe not just yet'.* His mind then fell on the policeman whose body he found, *'I wonder when his funeral is and why he has hardly been mentioned of late'.* He scoured away, looking for reports on the policeman, yet nothing, *'something isn't right here,'* he thought, *'the gang in London are all caught, 2 arrests in Liverpool for maybe having something to do with the robbery or handling of the items and 2 dead men, yet so little on the policeman, especially from the police themselves'.* He then noticed a small piece of news stating that the policeman's funeral is going to be held on Friday, *'ahh, should be more info coming out soon then on the news'.* He could feel his eyes getting heavy and knew he wasn't going to stay awake much longer, grabbing the lead he took Barney out for a late-night walk.

On his return he jumped straight into bed. As he lay there in his bed his mind drifted to think of his children and wondered what they would think of him in this situation and, god forbid, if he got found out. He then thought about his mum and dad and a smile came on his face as he could picture what his dad would say and it wouldn't have been good. He closed his eyes and drifted into a deep sleep.

15th April

Even though he wasn't at work he woke up at the usual time and got out of bed. He sat on the edge of the bed and he knew he still felt anxious, maybe it was the fear of being caught or simply that in the last few days he had left behind all his old routines and his brain was now working overtime on new ideas and new challenges and so seemed occupied constantly. The one thing he didn't like was change, but since finding the bag he had had to change and the nights of sitting there feeling sorry for himself, and at times missing his ex-wife, and the many nights of hating his ex-wife for doing this to him seem to have vanished overnight. As he washed his face this morning he thought once more of his ex-wife and, as always, he gave the expression of '*oh well, so be it,*' as he had known deep down it was never going to work but he still missed her face. But today he looked at himself in the mirror and said, "lost one old bag and found another," which brought a wry smile to his face.

The joker inside him was coming back out to play, he could always turn around a bad situation with a joke and kick on with his life and right here and now he felt the old him starting to come back. He headed down the stairs to make the 1st brew of the day and was greeted by Barney with the swaying dance he always did with his body moving from side to side and, as always, with a toy in his mouth. He petted him, then put him out in the garden, made a brew and joined Barney in the garden. He fed the birds and then had a his 1st roll up of the day and sat there and enjoyed the moment, it was a much nicer morning today and he scanned the garden and his plants. His thoughts then drifted back to the 2 policeman yesterday and he was glad he told them the truth about what day he was there, as a result it wouldn't have been suspicious or anything as there must have been loads of dog walkers and people using the path that same day. Barney was waiting at the gate for his morning walk but today he could wait a bit longer as he made another brew and sat there wondering what to do with his life now that he is 250 grand richer. In the last few days he has had thoughts from opening a business or maybe a trip to Las Vegas, in fact his thoughts have taken him to all sorts of places with the excitement of it all, but today his thoughts have come down to a more sobering view of it all, and again looking back at his past year and a half of being on his own with all the heartache and sadness, he went down that road once more just for the sake of it. The one thing he did notice today was that it didn't hurt anymore when he thought of his ex-wife, which was strange as even though he had hated the situation with her and her horror of a daughter the pain had gone, and yes he missed her face but that was it. He could clearly see her in his mind but it didn't hurt and he knew then that he had finally moved on and the days clinging on to a memory and an illusion of being happy together once more were over, though he still hated the daughter but he probably wasn't alone in that. It wasn't always the split from his wife that got him down as it was more that he had two marriages behind him, and he often reflected on what an idiot he was in the past and what a mess of his life he has made for himself, especially with his first wife and children. He sipped his tea only to realise it was cold, he must have been sitting there in a daze for a while just thinking of everything.

He quickly jumped up and took Barney out for a walk, his mind now thinking of what he should do next, the old saying 'all dressed up and nowhere to go' was coming to mind as he pondered on how to make a new start. One thing that was clear was that he had to keep his mind on the go as he felt totally revitalised over the last few days rather than the sluggish him of the last year, or the years of being trapped in a marriage of sadness. Now he was more like his old self again, switched on and full of fire, the fears of the last few days have subsided and, as each day passed. his confidence was growing, especially after facing his anxieties yesterday by walking the path and talking to the 2 policemen. Finally, on looking back at his marriage and feeling what he hoped he would feel many months before - nothing. He was wise enough to know that his emotions and feelings would be all over the place at times since his find but he also knew that this was the way forward and there was no turning back.

The 3 S's were now done and, on throwing some jeans and a top on, he made a fresh brew, sat in the garden, lit up a cig and looked at his plants with some pride as he relaxed. Looking at his watch it was now nearly 9am and he thought today would be as good a day as any to spend some of the cash.

Reaching into the loft he took out a bundle of cash and counted out 2 grand then jumped into his car and headed for Liverpool town centre as the shops there were fairly good, especially now with the new part of the town centre called Liverpool One. It had great shops and great places for a coffee and a bite to eat, he had often walked past some of these designer shops whilst en route to Matalan or

Primark but not today as he was walking in them, ready to buy.

Whilst driving into the town centre he felt excited as this was the 1st time he was going to spend some of the money he found and, yes, he felt there may be a slight risk, but since the money was used notes he should be fine, and he was actually enjoying the riskiness of it. Walking around the shops he thought how good it felt and let out a Bruce Almighty saying of "goood."

It wasn't long before he saw a shop with some quality suits, he had earlier split the 2K into 2 bundles so as not to pull all the money out in one go. The shop assistant came over and asked him if he could help and Shaun pointed out a few suits he liked. The assistant went into overdrive with his customer service which impressed Shaun, he normally paid up to 200 quid for a suit or, if it was for work, then 70 quid from Matalan, but this one today must have some sort of cotton in it as it was 480 quid. He tried the suit jacket on and the assistant brought him the trousers and when he put it all on it looked great, looked like it was made for him.

He stepped out the cubicle and the assistant came over and gave Shaun all the compliments he needed on how good he looked, "You suit dark blue, sir, it goes well with your skin tone."

"Oh, err, right, cheers mate," he replied, "I will take it, I could use a nice 16 and a half neck shirt with that too, and maybe a tie?"

The assistant went off and came back with a nice white shirt and a suitable tie, "This will go so well with that suit, sir."

In the past he had paid good money for some nice clothes but it had been a while. and following the assistant over to the counter he felt quite good, "I could use a pair of shoes as well to go with this suit, mate."

"Follow me, sir, I have just the shoes for a suit like this."

He told him his size and the assistant brought back a decent pair of shoes, "You will look the part with the suit and these shoes, sir."

He tried them on and they did feel great and looked great too, "OK, I will have them."

"Is that it, sir?"

"Yeah, that's it mate."

"Can you follow me to the pay desk please then, sir. How you paying, sir?"

"Err, I will pay cash, if you don't mind, I have a grand to spend today, I just hope I have enough left over to buy myself a coffee in a minute!"

The assistant laughed, "Well, sir, let's see what I can do, that's a total of £690 pounds, sir."

"Excellent, and thanks for your help today mate, your customer service was great."

The assistant was very happy with himself, probably with the sale, but maybe also with the nice comments on his customer service. Shaun counted out the money, handed it over to him and enjoyed the moment, "Thank you, sir, you will look fantastic in that suit. Have a great day, sir."

"You too, mate."

He walked outside and another 3 S's was created – *'Shirt, Suit and Shoes, we can forget the tie for now,'* he thought and smiled to himself, *'time for that coffee I think'*. As he strolled through the shopping complex he came across his favourite coffee hangout, *'ahh, Costa, this will do nicely'*. The Costa store was really nice inside and had some tables and chairs outside too which was a must for all smokers and people watchers. He grabbed his latte and picked a nice table outside where he sat himself down, rolled up a cig and enjoyed the moment of his 1st purchase. He sat back in his chair as the nicotine and caffeine did their thing and he felt really pleased with himself.

'That was fun,' he thought, *'and if I only spend average amounts in various places, then I won't stick out like a sore thumb or someone who has found a bag of cash!'* He looked down at his shoes and knew he could use a new pair of casual shoes too, so that was the next purchase. He took a sip from his coffee, and as he did a lady, maybe in her mid-forties, sat down on the next table to him. She looked very nice and caught Shaun's eye immediately, she had dark brown hair and dark brown eyes and dressed very well and, like him, had many bags of clothes shopping with her. Shaun couldn't help but notice she was not wearing a wedding ring, in fact, he found himself stealing another glance at her face. Not many woman have turned his head over the last year or so, and even then he would have ignored it as he was not ready for anyone else, but one glance at this lady has sent him into some sort of unexplored territory, and he could feel himself wanting to make a connection with this lady but didn't have a clue how to make an introduction or start a conversation. One thing Shaun could do was talk but he was quite shy at first in these type of matters, he turned his head around to steal

another glance at this woman, and as he did she smiled at him and asked him for a light for her cigarette. He quickly reached for his lighter and passed it to this wonderful looking lady, she lit her cigarette and thanked him and then she remarked about her shopping by saying she had one more item to get and she'd be done and out of here.

Shaun quickly replied, "I thought women loved clothes shopping."

"We do," she said, "or should I say, I do, but I need to get back home early today to pick my grandson up, otherwise I would shop till I drop."

Shaun laughed, "Well, I like shopping too, not too keen on all the crowds, but I love sitting down, having a coffee and watching all the people going past, so I tend to storm into town with some sort of plan and do the shopping I need and grab a coffee and then get the hell out of here."

She smiled and said, "Sounds a good idea and, like you, I love people watching too, I find it fascinating."

He couldn't help himself as the next words came out of his mouth, "My name is Shaun, what's yours?"

"Oh, my name is Kath."

"It's nice to meet you Kath."

"Likewise," said Kath.

He could feel the nerves building up inside him, but even by his own silly standards she was a good 8 plus, he quickly said, "Am looking for a good pair of casual shoes or boots next, something to go with a pair of jeans."

"Shoe shopping is a speciality for me," she replied.

"Ohh, am hopeless am afraid when it comes to shoes Kath."

"Doesn't your wife help you when you shop?"

"Am on my own now Kath, it's been about a year and a half."

"Oh, am sorry," she said.

"No its OK, Kath, it was definitely for the best, just takes some getting used to being on your own, how about you?"

"Am single too now," Kath replied, "I've been divorced for about 2 years and I wholeheartedly agree with you that it takes some getting used to being on your own."

Shaun quickly came back with, "Have you tried seeing anyone again?"

"I've thought about it, Shaun, but between work and looking after my grandkids it's too difficult to find the time to meet someone, how about you Shaun?"

"No, not seeing anyone, to be truthful the first 6 months I didn't know what was going to happen and then I found out my ex was seeing someone else and I knew then it was over, and for the next few months just tried to get to grips with the fact it's over. I have thought a lot about meeting someone else more recently but probably too scared to venture out there again, and when you're on your own for a while it's easier to stay that way, but I do miss the company of woman."

"Well, Shaun, it's been lovely chatting to you and I wish you well, but I have to get back to the grandkids and I still have to get a top for the little lad."

Shaun thought he had messed up with the reply of 'I do miss the company of a woman', but looked at Kath and said, "It's been fantastic talking to you."

Kath stood up, picked her bags up, smiled at him and said goodbye, Shaun wanted to call after her but knew he could have done better with his words than 'I do miss the company of a woman', but it's true, as he did.

Kath then stopped dead in her tracks, turned around, walked back over to Shaun and said, "You could do with trying the shop just around the corner from here for your shoes," and pointed to where the shop was.

"Hang on," said Shaun, "I will get my bags and you can guide me to the shop as am hopeless at directions too."

She laughed and said, "It's a good job I stopped off for a coffee, otherwise you would be walking round forever looking for them shoes!"

As they got to the store she told him he would find all the shoes he would need there and, quick as a flash, Shaun took out his pen, wrote his mobile number on a receipt, gave it to Kath and said, "I know it sounds crazy, Kath, but if you fancy another coffee sometime, then give us a call."

He put out his hand with the receipt and she took it and said, "You may need this receipt in case you need to take something back."

He then quickly came back with, "Well, more reason to call me then, eh!"

"Thank you, Shaun, and take care."

Kath walked away and he watched her walk into the distance, he felt like a teenager again, all nerves and that funny feeling inside. Picking up his bags he walked into the shoe shop and, as Kath said, he found everything he needed in there and bought himself a pair of shoes and a good pair of boots. He paid the assistant £230 for the shoes, left the shop and headed for the car with all his bags of goodies. The money and the clothes all seemed immaterial as his only thoughts whilst walking to his car were of Kath and her lovely dark brown hair and eyes, and wondering if she would call his number. The walk to the car took no time at all and he filled the boot of his car with all today's purchases, then he fired up his car and drove home. Shaun was a happy man and he listened to his music and sang to it as he drove home.

On getting home he took out all the bags and put them away, then made a big fuss of Barney and a brew. He headed into the garden and checked his phone in case any messages awaited him but, alas, nothing. He rolled up a cig and took in his day and how great it felt with his new-found wealth and how amazing it felt to meet this lady. A week earlier this would not have happened as he was too low and had no confidence at all and even if Kath sat down next to him, he would not have said a word, but since finding the bag that day with the money and the diamonds, it has turned his life around and has given him a new drive and energy and he felt more like the old Shaun and not the one that was hidden inside himself for so long and silently thanked god for the bag.

He went back inside the house and pulled out what money he had left and realised he had spent over £900, *'geez, that was easy spending,'* he thought, *'and not spending too much to make a difference and stand out'*. But it was making a big difference to Shaun, people close to him had already seen a difference and the new suits etc. would certainly be noticed with his family, as he spent most of the last year with hardly any money and what money he did have was taken up by monstrous gas and electricity bills as his little house was like a freezer in the winter, *'but I guess a few new items could be masked over,'* he thought. There were many times in the last year he had thought about changing his image and he often spoke to his work colleague, Katie, about doing this, as for most of his life he had been a rocker, and still to this day he saw himself as an aging rocker. He hadn't a clue about what type of clothes to buy and Katie would help him when it came to buying new clothes, but when she sees him with the new suit and shoes etc. she will ask him about them and think that maybe Shaun doesn't need her help anymore. He would have to say to her, "Look what you started!" and get her involved and then maybe it may seem more normal to be buying stuff on his own. Looking at his watch it was nearly 3pm and, after looking at his plants and seeing they were starting to come along nicely, he decided to get back into the car and drive up to the garden centre for some more very nice plants.

Whilst he was there he bought a 3 tier garden box for £100. He couldn't believe how expensive it was, but he knew that when he finished placing some trailing lobelia and some other flowers in the tiers it would create a blanket of colour from top to bottom which would look fantastic. He picked up some more pots and flowers and arrived at the till with a huge smile on his face.

"We can deliver the garden boxes tomorrow after 4, if that's OK?"

"Yeah, that's fine," said Shaun.

He paid the money and then started to fill his car with all the pots and flowers he had bought, he had so many flowers that he had to place some on the back seat and front passenger seat, *'God help what other motorists will think when they see me going past, as it looks like a greenhouse on wheels!'*

He checked his phone again, but nothing. He reflected on what Kath had told him about picking up the grandkids and thought the chance of a call or message now would be zero, as she would have her hands full with them. He could see her face in his mind and he liked that face so much, there was something very special about her and it stirred all his emotions when he looked into those big brown eyes of hers, *'geez, pull yourself together man,'* he thought, as his mind was going into overdrive whilst he sat in the car park of the garden centre, *'I better make my way home,'* he thought.

He took the plants home, got them all out the car, put them in some sort of order to sort out and gave them a good watering. He started to place them into bigger pots and used the compost he had in the shed, which he had known would come in handy sooner or later when he bought that much a few weeks ago, which was another thing he did a lot - buying more than what he needed when it came to gardening as you never know when you would need more. He had all the lobelias, petunias and other smaller trays put to one side, waiting for his new 3 tier garden box delivery the next day, and finished off planting and sorting out what he could. *'This will look great in a few weeks' time,'* he thought.

He went for a quick wash and then grabbed the lead and took Barney for a walk.

It wasn't long before he bumped into another dog walker and they chatted for several minutes. As he left them and walked around the corner he saw the old woman who must walk her dog a 100 times a day, she was a lovely old woman who had all her wits about her and, after looking after his own elderly mum for the last 10 years of his life, he always gave the old woman some of his time and listened to her tales about her dog and, not forgetting, the latest gossip from the neighbourhood as she didn't miss a trick. Carrying on his walk he heard the ringtone of a text message coming from his phone, reaching into his pocket at the speed of light to see who it was from, hoping it was Kath, but, alas, it wasn't, but it was his lovely daughter, Laura. She was asking how he was, so when he got to the place where he could let Barney off the lead he called his daughter and told her about his day and all about Kath.

"You little charmer, Dad, what are you like, eh?"

"Well, Laura, your Dad has still got it kid."

"Well, Dad, if she does call you back, I may agree with you!"

"Listen, Laura, I will pop up and see you and my lovely little grandson tomorrow, if that's OK?"

"Yeah, Dad, that's great. See ya tomorrow, and I hope she calls."

"Yeah, me too. Ta ra baby."

He sat there and thought about his grandson, then went down memory lane thinking of his own mum and how much he missed her since her death 4 years ago and what he wouldn't give to get one more smile from her face. She had always made him feel special and loved, and in the last 2 years of a marriage breakdown and now living on his own for the first time he wished he could somehow share his feelings with his mum once more. He thought about how he felt when his mum was alive - he always felt like a kid with her alive and only when she died did he feel it was time to grow up. At 50 that felt kind of strange, as not having your parents around you makes you feel so different. He had spent the last few years of her life looking after her and was happy that he did as she had needed him due to her illness, but she was strong too, and he got to know his mum like he never had before. When she died, a big part of him died too. He had got married soon after, but the grief was still there and, coupled with a marriage destined for failure, his life had been going downhill fast. He knew he was now getting stronger, the hurt of the last few years was moving away, the little house he lived in wasn't ideal in some ways, but it had helped him sort himself out. Grabbing the lead and calling Barney over, he walked him back and thought about all the changes in his life over the last few years and shook his head.

On getting home it was time for something to eat. He opted for a quick fix of a microwave chicken masala and rice meal, which always tasted quite good for a microwave meal. He fed Barney and as the microwave finished, he took the meal out and put it out on a plate. He cut some crusty bread to go with it and got stuck in. As he was halfway through it his phone went off again, he reached over, looked and, to his astonishment, it was Kath! Her text read: *"If you want your receipt back, then I will be in the same Costa Coffee tomorrow at 11! Kath."*

His face was a picture as he punched the air in delight and shouted something stupid like, "Get Paid!"

He calmed himself down and replied saying: *"An excellent idea, though you may have to show me around some more shops :] Shaun."*

Kath's reply was instant: *"Deal, cya tomoz Kath x"*

'Oh my God, what is happening to me? From zero to hero in 5 days, money coming out of my ears and now a lady who is out of my wildest dreams.'

He left his dinner to head straight to the kettle and made a brew. On making his tea, he went out into the garden and rolled a cig. Puffing at his cig, he still couldn't comprehend all the events of the last 5 days, he texted his daughter in bold capitals: *"SHE TEXT!"*

Laura's reply said: *"Way to go Dad, don't mess it up, be yourself x."*

She was right, he had to be his self, but the crazy thing was that he wasn't too sure who he was lately… but nothing on earth was going to stop him trying tomorrow.

Going back into the house and looking at his cold meal he decided it was a time of celebration so he headed off to KFC. He drove there, sitting in the car park and eating his hot wings like a man who has never eaten before as his hunger was now incredible. He listened to the radio for any further news but nothing. His KFC was now eaten and, as he sipped on his diet coke, he rolled up another cig, sat back in his car seat and thought of his day and how the feeling of being uneasy yesterday had now moved on to a sense of excitement and anticipation.

On getting home he couldn't settle at all so he took Barney out for a quick walk. As he did, a blue car passed him that was just like his ex-wife's and he quickly looked to see if it was her, but it wasn't, *'that's all I would need,'* he thought, *'if she walked back into my life now… yes, I still care about her but my time with her is done'.*

On getting home he switched on the TV and sat down to watch it, but found his mind wandering between the money and the lady he met for 20 minutes today that has him now on a string. But then he had a more sobering thought of being on guard so as not to slip with the money and diamonds, as he knew his life would be transformed again then, this time via Her Majesty's Pleasure. He sat on his PC and looked for any further news on the heist and shootings but nothing. That story seemed to have come and gone.

The night quickly came around and he took himself off to bed. As he lay there he thanked God for the money and thanked him for the chance meeting with someone who, unlike anyone else that year, had given him the feeling of want and desire again. For the past year, he had hoped that one day he would wake up and all the sadness and heartache would be gone, but it just didn't happen, as each day he would find a reminder in his mind of how it was and how it could have been and how it was now. It takes a lot of soul searching, but the hardest thing for him was the being alone and the feeling of failure and distrust and kicking himself for not listening to his true feelings before he married that woman. He pictured Kath's face in his mind and relived the few moments he had with her and smiled to himself. He thought about how much his life had changed and how upbeat he felt since finding the bag, and how circumstances can change so quickly, especially when least expected, but finding the bag had somehow drawn him to meet Kath and he had a date tomorrow that nothing on this earth was going to stop him attending. He closed his eyes and started to drift into a deep sleep and his last words to God were an instruction to look after him.

16ᵗʰ April

His eyes opened and he immediately looked at his phone and switched off the alarm, once again, a few minutes before it was due to go off. He still felt tired and sat up against the bed. His first thoughts were of Kath and the meet up later today and then his thoughts came to an abrupt stop when Barney came running into the bedroom with his toy in his mouth to greet him. For a 10 year old dog, he still was like a puppy at times. Shaun looked at Barney and said, "OK mate, down the stairs we go."

Barney skipped down the spiral staircase, turning his head every few steps to make sure Shaun was following him, then went straight to the front door. "What's up Barnes? You dying for a wee, mate?"

The answer was given the second he opened the door and Barney ran straight to his favourite place in the garden to relieve himself, "Good boy, lad."

Making a brew and sitting outside in the garden. he thought about the day ahead and rolled up the 1st cig of the day. Normally, he would spend this time shifting through the emails on his phone and focusing on his work, but work simply didn't seem to exist this last week as the roller coaster of events was simply massive.

He took Barney out for a walk and noticed that the normally cold air was starting to feel that bit warmer, reminding him that summer was just around the corner. He let Barney off the lead and thought some more about the bag and its contents, especially the diamonds. He shook his head as he still didn't know what on earth to do with them, *'what if I had got caught.'* he thought, *'geez, stop it, Shaun. I didn't get caught and I was careful and am hopefully on a home run now'*.

He brought Barney back home and got ready to meet up with Kath. He jumped into the shower and had a shave, using a new blade to make sure he had a totally smooth face. He finished the 3 S's, made another brew, plonked himself down behind the PC, and navigated the web for anything new on the shootings and the heist, mainly for anything local that could incriminate him, but the only interesting news was of the policeman's funeral which would be tomorrow. Reading through the article it was clear the police hadn't given any details about why he was there at the time of his killing and, interestingly, the funeral was for friends and family only, *'seems strange not having a big police send-off, especially with being killed on duty! Oh well, maybe that's the way the family wanted it'*. He sat there for a while, pondering everything he had just read and feeling more confident that he has got the bag and no one saw him. But still that strange feeling started to come back over him, *'maybe it's the thought of the dead policeman,'* he thought, *'or if I get caught with the money and the diamonds, I may be having an early funeral too!'* The last 3 days he had felt anxious and today was no different, except that he had a very important date to attend and he was excited at the thought of meeting her again, but this strange feeling just wouldn't go away. *'Fuck's sake,'* he thought, *'what the hell is it?'* Was it the find or the funeral? Or maybe that he was letting go of his old life and starting a new chapter… whatever it was, he didn't like the feeling that was inside him, *'pull yourself together man,'* he thought, *'there's nothing wrong!'* To some people these feelings probably didn't amount to much, but with Shaun he listened to his body and always took its messages very seriously, the last time he had had feelings like this was the day he was walking up his old road where he lived with his mum and, every day, when he got to the top of the road he would turn left to go to the shops. That day as he got there he decided to turn right for some strange reason and go the longer way, all because he had had a strange feeling, that feeling that day saved his life, as if he had turned left as normal, he would have been hit by a car that veered off the road and smashed into the wall where he would have been. There were many other incidents, though none as severe as that one. He had often talked to people close to him about some of these strange events and called it a sixth sense or simply coincidence, but over the years he had learnt to trust his feelings and gut instinct. Suddenly, grabbing his coat, he jumped into the car and headed off to the town centre.

On parking the car, he walked towards Costa Coffee. He checked his watch and saw he was 30 minutes early so, on passing a music shop, he decided to call in and buy a Rammstein CD, which he would play extremely loudly on the way home if all went well today.

On arrival at Costa he could feel his heart beating faster as he waited for Kath. He sat himself down at a table and looked through all the crowds of people to see where she was. He caught sight of her and watched her walk towards him, he admired how she looked, every inch a lady. He stood up and smiled and she waved as she got closer. He leaned forward and kissed her on the cheek, and as he did he closed his eyes for a split second, as the fragrance she was wearing smelt so nice.

"Hey, hello you!" Kath said in a playful tone.

"Hiya Kath, I got a good table for us, what would you like to drink, and would you like anything to eat?"

"Mocha for me and no food just yet," she replied, "but maybe later, eh?"

"OK then, a mocha, and a latte for me."

He ordered the coffees and brought them back out. As he placed the coffees on the table Shaun said, "It doesn't seem like a day has passed, now that we are sitting down together again. So, how did it go with the grandkids?"

"Oh, they're good lads. As long as you keep them entertained, they're always good," Kath looked at Shaun and continued, "I don't know what you must think of me from asking you for a light and then meeting you again today, as that's not what I would normally do!"

He smiled at Kath and said, "Well, am glad you did, and it's a first for me too, though I did think just by looking at you that you looked the type of person that couldn't let a man down who needed a good pair of shoes!"

She laughed, "So that's it, eh? Did you get a pair?"

"*A* pair," quipped Shaun, "I got *2* pairs, and am wearing a pair now."

She looked and said, "Yes, they're nice, they go well with your jeans."

"Thanks Kath, so did you manage to get a top for your grandson?"

"Yes and, like you, I got 2 tops for him as they were a bargain."

He couldn't stop looking into Kath's eyes as he was definitely under her spell. They spoke for a while longer whilst they enjoyed the coffee and he asked Kath if she would like to walk to the waterfront.

"Yes, that would be nice, as there are some lovely views from there," replied Kath.

As they strolled towards the waterfront it was clear that the 2 of them were very happy spending time together. Shaun told her a story from when he was a boy and he used to come down to this very same place, though it all looked very different then as the old docks were closed and the big warehouses and cobbled streets were empty, and he and his friends used to go on the rooftops of some of the old buildings to collect bird eggs. He and his friends would sit for hours on these old dockyard buildings, just gazing across the River Mersey.

"It's hard to believe how it all used to be around here, especially now that some of the buildings have been all done up and restored."

Kath replied, "At least some ships have returned to the dockyards."

They called into a pub, ordered drinks and took them outside where they gazed over the view of the Mersey as they both shared stories from their lives. He was hooked on every word Kath said and couldn't help notice how attractive she was, she told him she was 47 but if she had said 37, he would have believed her as her skin was beautiful and she had such a youthful face and a figure that made him want her. They sipped at their drinks and they lit up a cig, and as he gave her his lighter she held his hand briefly and looked straight into Shaun's eyes.

"Am so glad we met today, Shaun. It's been a while since I've enjoyed myself like this, I spend so much time working and looking after my grandkids that time for just me is so rare."

"So what do you do, Kath? For work?"

"Oh, am a personal assistant for a small law firm in Manchester, what about you, Shaun?"

Shaun told her about his job carrying out risk assessments and accident investigations, "Keeps me on my toes," he said, "though I've taken some leave this week, which is the best decision I've made in a long time as I've met you, Kath."

"Ha, you sweet talker," she replied, "I have taken the week off too, but mainly to help out with my daughter and the grandkids."

"So, how many grandkids you got then?"

"Oh, just the 2. One is 3 years old and the other is 5."

Shaun told Kath about his grandkids and the conversation just flowed.

Kath's phone rang and she said, "Oh, it's my daughter, I wonder what she wants?"

She answered the phone and listened to what her daughter was saying, her face looked anxious as she was listening and responded to her daughter, "No, it's OK, I will come straight over," as she put the phone away.

Shaun asked her if everything was all right.

"No, not really. Shaun, I am going to have to go home now, my daughter needs me, but I would love to see you again."

"Yes, me too, Kath, I hope all is OK when you get home."

"Yeah, I hope so too," she replied, "am parked the other side of the town so I better get a taxi to it, I'm so sorry to cut our day so short, Shaun."

As she stood up it was clear that she needed to go straight away, she walked up to Shaun, placed her arms around him, kissed him gently on the lips and said, "Thank you for the day, I'll call you later this evening to explain."

Shaun flagged down a taxi and Kath got in and then she was gone.

He sat himself down on a bench nearby and lit up a cig, he was delighted at the way it went but wished the day could have lasted longer. He licked his lips as he could still taste her lipstick on his mouth and sat there enjoying the moment, not having a care in the world as others walked by to see him sitting on the bench with a huge smile on his face.

He then strolled back towards the town centre where he called into a fragrance shop and bought himself some more of his favourite aftershave, Kokorico, and then called into Costa for another coffee before the drive home as he had had a glass of lager earlier and he knew the dangers of driving under the influence, no matter how small the quantity. But, in truth, any excuse for a hit of caffeine worked for him, normally it was Costa for him but Caffè Nero ran a close second. As he sat there and enjoyed the coffee he felt totally energised and happy, and the happiness he had found with the money in the bag couldn't compare to the happiness he now felt with Kath. Meeting Kath had lifted him to greater heights and two short spaces of time were enough for him to realise how much he liked this lady. Sitting there drinking his coffee he wondered what had happened with her daughter to make her leave so quickly and hoped she was nothing like his ex-wife's daughter who, he was convinced, was spawned by the devil and used people for her own gain, *'but I doubt there are 2 people like her in this world,'* he hoped. He finished his coffee and checked his watch - it was just after 2 pm so he had only been with Kath a few hours but it had seemed like it was only minutes.

He got to his car and sent Kath a text message saying: **"Thank you for the day it was beautiful and I hope your daughter is OK x."**

Whilst driving home a text alert came in and he pulled over to check his phone. It was Kath and read: **"Shaun it was a beautiful day and am so sorry to cut it short, please call me after 8 tonight. Kath x."** Driving the rest of the way home he now knew she liked him too, as for a split second before he had thought that maybe she had arranged the great escape with her daughter in case things weren't working out well to save her from him!

On getting home, Barney gave him the usual welcome of a toy in his mouth. He clipped the lead on Barnes and took him out for a quick walk. The weather had just started to turn and some light rain had started to fall but Shaun didn't care as he was a happy man. He met up with some other dog walkers and discussed the usual stuff of dog flees and pet grooming; Shaun could never understand all the effort some people go to with dogs and, yes, every now and again he would wash Barney and get the old flea spray out, but he was lucky that Barney never needed grooming except for a quick brush every now and again. The lady in question who he was talking too lived her life for her dog, *'but I guess that's easy to do when you live on your own as Barney gets treated like royalty by me too and am guilty of talking too much to him'*. As he walked away from that lady and her dog he then walked straight into the old neighbourhood watch lady and her dog too, and he knew he would be spending the next 10 minutes listening to her as he could never get a word in edgeways with her unless she asked him a question - and even then she finished off the sentence for him!

She eventually asked him why he wasn't at work and, before he could finish his sentence, she said, "Are you taking some leave from work?" and then burst in again saying, "yes. I noticed your car there each day and wondered why you wasn't in work."

"Yeah, I met a friend in town today for a coffee," Shaun replied and he knew the second he had said this he had just thrown some fuel into the fire with this old lady.

"Oh, a friend! A lady friend! Ohh, that's the best bit of being single when you're younger!" she exclaimed and told him about her younger days when she was single.

'Guess I will be talk of the neighbourhood now,' he thought. "Well, she is only a friend, nothing serious," he said aloud, "anyways, I better get going as the rain is getting heavier now," he added and walked away in large strides to pull well clear of her. Barney pulled hard on the lead too to get away, he had obviously had enough gossip as well.

Eventually getting home, he put the kettle on and made a brew and a few ham butties and Barney helped him eat them too. He got a text from his daughter asking: ***"Can we meet up tomorrow rather than later."*** He texted back saying that was fine, and said he had met Kath and it went great. Laura replied: ***"Hey Dad fantastic x."***

Whilst drinking his tea he realised he hadn't given the bag any thought in the last few hours, which was a welcome break as it had been on his mind 24/7 since he found it, as all he has wanted to do is meet Kath and talk to her again. But he had to wait till 8 o clock to talk to her and so decided to get a quick shower as he still felt slightly anxious and a bit stressed out.

Stepping into the shower he let the warm water do its job as the water dripped down his face and, with his 2 hands against the wall, he let the shower do its magic as it eased his stress.

He was just getting dressed when a knock came at his door, *'shit I wonder who this is?'* He came down the stairs and opened the door, he was half expecting the police but it was the delivery man with his 3-tier garden box, "Cheers mate, just put it in the garden please," he told him.

He quickly threw on some old jeans and a top and set to work with his new gardening boxes. It wasn't long before he had it all set up and all the plants he had bought yesterday in their places, all he needed now was some warmer weather and some tender loving care and he would have a garden to be proud of. *'A quick wash to get the soil off of my fingers and hands and then a bite to eat,'* he thought.

He set about making some tea and, rather than make a ready meal, he opted for a chicken stir fry and made himself a very nice meal.

After he had eaten his meal he went back outside to drink his brew and light up a cig and enjoyed looking at his new 3 tier garden boxes. It was nearly 8 pm and he could feel the excitement of talking to Kath, *'geez, am like a school kid here,'* he thought as the nerves kicked in more.

He waited till just after 8 to make the call as he felt if he made it dead on 8, that would make her freak out as he was too keen, but that's the way he did feel as he was sweet on her. Hitting the call button on the phone he sat down and waited for her to answer,

"Hey."

"Hiya Shaun."

"Hello you," he replied, "it was great today, been thinking of you all day since."

"Ahh, thanks, Shaun, I have been thinking of you all day too and cannot wait to see you again. I only wish I could see you tomorrow, but unfortunately I cannot as I have to go to a funeral with my daughter."

"Oh, am sorry to hear that, Kath."

"Yeah Shaun, that's why I had to go today as my daughter got very upset. She lost her partner last week and is dreading the funeral tomorrow."

"Yeah, I can imagine Kath. How did her partner die? If you don't mind me asking!"

"He was killed last week, Shaun."

"Hey!! Killed Kath? What happened?"

"Yeah, Shaun. It's been all over the news, he was shot last week by criminals in West Derby."

Shaun was speechless and felt like he had been shot too, his mind became a total blank as Kath continued to explain what had happened to her daughter's policeman partner.

"You still there, Shaun? Shaun?!"

Shaun hit the end call button and shouted a few obscenities across the room... and then further obscenities, *'shit, shit, what is going on, this is insane,'* he thought and he kept repeating shit as his phone starting to ring again. Shaun's face was riddled with anxiety and confusion as he answered the phone.

"Hi Shaun, I lost you there."

"Oh, it's my phone, Kath, sorry about that, I always lose my signal in the house. I've just walked into the garden to hear you better," he lit a cig, pulled hard on the roll up and tried to gain as much composure as possible, "I read all about that shooting, Kath, sounds terrible."

"My daughter has taken it bad Shaun, she is distraught with it all, though, Shaun, I have to say, and this may sound awful, but am not that upset at all by it as I didn't like him one bit. If we can meet up on Saturday, I will fully explain to you why as my daughter is in the next room now so I cannot speak freely."

"Yeah, that's fine Kath, no problem at all."

"Why don't we meet up outside the Costa place Shaun, say around 5pm, and we can go for a bite to eat and I will explain it all?"

"Yeah, that sounds great Kath, let me know how it goes tomorrow and maybe we can have a quick chat tomorrow night if you feel up to it."

"OK Shaun, thanks again for a lovely day and I will see you soon, take care."

"You too, Kath."

On putting the phone down he sat motionless on the sofa with his head in his hands, none of it felt real, "How on earth has this happened, what is going on?!" he shouted loudly.

Walking into the back kitchen he put the kettle on, as if a brew would help him make sense of it all. *'Oh my God, this is insane,'* he thought to himself as he sipped on his tea. He went into the garden and lit up a cig, this was too much to take in and he sat staring at the grass and shaking his head, the bag that has changed his life hasn't finished with him just yet he thought, *'the finding of the bag was one thing, but now finding the mother of the daughter whose partner was killed trying to get away with the bag is another thing. How on earth could this happen to me, of all the people in Liverpool to meet I find the one who is tied up with the bag, am going to have to walk away from her as I couldn't live a lie, every time I would look at her daughter, or speak to Kath about it, I would be lying through my back teeth to conceal that I had come across him and took what he was carrying and got the money and the diamonds that her partner died for and didn't do nothing about it except run and keep them for my selfish self.'* It was too late to save her partner as he was well dead when he found the bag but it still wouldn't go down well with Kath or her daughter saying "well, all isn't lost as I have his money and diamonds!" His mind wondered about the bag itself and

85

whether it was, in a strange way, bringing them together for a reason, like some sort of spiritual power doing its thing, *'naah, that's too weird to even imagine,'* he thought, *'but it was strange, as if it wasn't for the bag, I would never have met Kath, but now it's a bit too close for comfort'*. He felt like crying as he didn't want to let go of Kath but knew this would eventually cause problems and he couldn't lie to her or hide something like that away from her, plus it put him at risk too.

Even though it was still early he locked up the house, went to bed, and lay there thinking of it all. He knew that he should walk away but how could fate be so cruel and deal him a hand like this, he had just come from a failed 2nd marriage and a year and a half of not wanting anyone else till he had seen her face. All the months of trying to understand what went wrong and the months of anger, followed by acceptance, was something he didn't want to go through again and he thought he was destined to be on his own the rest of his life until a faint glow of light which was now flickering and he was now about to put the flame out without feeling the warmth from its glow and using this light to see through the darkness. It made sense to let her go, but just like the diamonds which he should of got rid of right from the start but couldn't let them go simply because of their beauty and worth, he didn't want to let Kath go for the same reasons. He lay there and pictured Kath's face in his mind and, as he did, his phone text went off. It was Kath, *'geez woman, you know when am thinking of you too!'* The text simply read: ***"Nite Shaun xx."*** He couldn't help himself and rather than ignore the text he replied: ***"Am thinking of you, Nite lovely x."*** One of his favourite films called 'Heat' with Robert DeNiro had a saying in it which was: "the minute you feel the heat you walk away." *'How* *right he was,'* he thought, but then he thought of what his mother use to say to him as a lad and that was: "if you want something in life, then go for it." His mother was very seldom wrong too, but DeNiro made sense. Shaun has had a difficult time over the last 12 years with looking after his elderly mum with dementia until her death and then a marriage of hell and then a year and a half of trying to find himself again and now a new start in life, which seemed to be what he has longed for, now seemed to be in tatters once more. He thought about the anxiousness he had felt the last few days and he had been taking it as a warning, but maybe this was his sixth sense building up to the meeting of Kath.

He lay there tossing and turning all night and thinking of the strange set of events that has unfolded: the delight in finding the bag to the shock of finding the body, and then deciding to spend some of the money to find a woman that stole his heart within a few seconds of meeting. *'It is so strange, but to find out she is connected to the bag is just unreal'*. The hours passed until he eventually fell asleep, exhausted.

17th April

He opened his eyes and he gazed at the phone for the time, it was nearly 6am. He knew he had had enough sleep and so got up and hit the bathroom. He came down the stairs, greeted Barney, put the kettle on and made a brew. He took it out into the garden with Barney, his mind was already deep in thought as he sipped his tea, "Geez, its freezing," he said to Barney and ran back in to put a coat and hat on.

He went back outside and finished off his tea and a roll up, he fed the birds and then, before he knew it, he was heading back into the kitchen to make a 2nd brew. His mind cast back to the dead policeman he had found, which he tried hard to block out of his mind till then, and then, as he briefly thought last night, thought again that somehow the bag that brought him this new lease of life and brought him and Kath together. Was it playing some sort of strange game with him or was it the dead policeman's spirit guiding him back towards her daughter, *'geez, that's too fucking weird,'* he thought to himself, *'but it's strange, in fact very strange, no wonder I had all those feelings'.* Shaun had often talked to Barney, but had found in the last few days he was talking more to himself, as if to try reasoning with himself, and today was no exception from that as he babbled out words of frustration. As he finished his 2nd brew he noticed Barney waiting by the gate and waiting for him to take him for a walk but he didn't feel like going for a walk this morning as his head was totally wrecked and his legs felt heavy. Barney was staring into Shaun's eyes with his tail wagging, "Bloody hell Barnes, come on then, let's go out," he grabbed the lead and took Barney out, even with all these strange events happening and his head all mashed up he gave out a little laugh and continued, "Barney, you're a pain in the bloody arse, mate."

Barney just kept on walking, he didn't care about how cold and horrible it was today, or that his owner was like the living dead this morning. He got to the part where he could let Barney off the lead and sat himself down and had a cig whilst Barney sniffed and pissed against every tree in sight. Eventually he did a number 2 and out came the poop bag and as he scooped it up his fingers went through the bag, "Oh, for fuck's sake!" he shouted as he looked down at his fingers covered in dog shit.

Even Barney stopped dead in his tracks when he shouted, Shaun counted to 10 to calm himself down, put the bag inside another bag and, as he had no tissues with him, he had to wipe his hands on the damp grass, *'I just hope I don't meet anyone on the way back,'* he thought. He walked back home at the speed of light to wash his hands, even Barney could hardly keep up, and on getting back home he headed straight to the bathroom, got some soap and hot water, and scrubbed his hands till he was totally convinced they were clean. *'There is an old saying that if you stand in dog muck, then it brings good luck, I just hope it applies to fingers too!'* After he had scrubbed his hands he got into the shower and let the hot water do its magic as it soothed his body and relieved the tension he had this morning. He thought of Kath's face and, from being cold due to the miserable weather this morning, he now felt warm and much better. Stepping out of the shower he was still picturing Kath's face and as he dried himself he sat on the edge of the bath and said loudly, "Am not letting her go, let's see this through."

He thought if this was fate doing its thing, then maybe, just maybe, he may be all right, as he hadn't been caught by the police with the find of the bag so it could possibly work out with Kath! He knew the thought of fate doing its thing was just papering over the cracks but that's all he had this morning, he simply didn't want to lose her. He was normally a master of disguise when it came to hiding his feelings and always searched for positives even when there seemed no hope at all, but all he did know was that he wanted to be with Kath again. He went upstairs and had a shave then when all bathroom duties were done he put on some warmer casual clothes and made a fresh brew.

By now it was just after 8am and he checked his phone for messages but none. Sitting with his brew he typed in a text message to Kath saying: ***"Thinking of you and your daughter on this sad day"***, *'naah that's rubbish,'* he thought and typed in: ***"If you need anyone to talk to today Kath, then I am here for you xx"*** and hit the send button. After a few minutes his phone rang and it was Kath.

"Hey."

"Hello Kath, how's you?"

"I'm glad you text Shaun, I've been up since so early this morning and I cannot stop thinking of you."

"Ahh, that's nice, Kath, and, like you, I've been up since really early too and I must have thought of you nearly every second."

"Hey Shaun, I know this may sound crazy as I've only met you twice, but I miss you, you have made me feel really good about myself again."

Shaun replied saying he felt the same and how lovely it feels when he is close to her.

"And here was me thinking you put something in my coffee Shaun!"

"Ha, yeah, well I had to Kath, instant love pill I think they call it!"

She laughed and said, "Well, whatever it was, it's still working Shaun, listen can I call you tonight when all the funeral etc. is over?"

"Yeah, sure Kath, I'd like that, cannot wait."

"OK then Shaun. Well, have a good day and I will catch you later."

"Yeah, talk soon Kath, and I hope the day goes as well as things could in them situations."

"Thanks Shaun, ta-ra babe."

Shaun was smitten and he knew it and the call confirmed to him that he couldn't let her go and he had to see her again even though he had 250000 reasons not to. Looking around the living room he thought maybe it could do with a bit of a clean, especially now, as soon he may be having a guest around! Putting all the stuff back in the right places and throwing out a lot of stuff he simply didn't need, he got stuck in with the cleaning and it helped make the morning go by quicker. He blitzed the living room and then the kitchen, had a quick brew and then did the bathroom and by the time he got to the bedroom he was wasted, *'geez, this is hard bloody work, why don't I do this more often?'* he thought, *'to save doing it like this, I should keep on top of it'*. Making another brew he sat outside to cool down, rolled up a cig and thought about Kath and the funeral, *'not nice funerals, not nice at all'*.

After his cig he opted for a drive to the supermarket and picked up a cooked chicken, some tiger bread and a potato salad from Sainsbury's. Whilst he was there he had a lengthy chat with the assistant on the bread aisle as they had changed the name from tiger bread to giraffe bread, the assistant explained that some young girl with her mum said that it looked more like a giraffe with its crusty colours than a tiger so they should call it giraffe bread and they decided to do just that.

"Well, let's hope the little girl doesn't want to change the name of that chocolate mousse you sell as that looks like shit!"

The assistant just gave him a look and shook her head, she obviously wasn't in a good mood today. He walked away and was sorry he had asked her.

On getting home he and Barney had a chicken feast complete with the, err, giraffe bread. Afterwards he jumped on the PC and looked for any further news on anything, there were a few articles on the funeral but, as always, no real news about it. He then went upstairs and climbed into the loft and just sat up there looking at the money in the bag and then taking the box with the diamonds and sat there admiring their beauty, even in this low light they sparkled like little stars in the night sky, and he was starting to understand why some people would do anything to get them. As he put them away he stared at the gun and looked at what sort it was, it was a Glock 19 handgun and when he got down from the loft he had a quick check on the net about the gun, *'hmm, seems popular, this gun, with just about everyone from the police to your average gun fanatic'.* Just as he was about to read some more on this killing machine the phone rang, it was his daughter.

"Hey baby, all OK?"

"Yeah, fine Dad, what time you popping up to see us?"

"Oh, I can be there in 30 minutes, if that's OK?"

"Yeah, great Dad, cya then."

He stood up and wasn't happy with himself at all as he had completely forgotten about going up to see her and the grandson. Quickly sorting himself out he jumped in the car and drove up to see her.

When he got there, he made a big fuss over his grandson and his daughter and she said, "Well, Dad?"

"Err, well what, babe?"

"Kath, Dad!"

"Ohh… err…"

"Come on Dad, spill the beans, how's it going with her?"

He told his daughter everything and she said, "Dad, am so happy for you, just don't rush things as I don't want to see you get hurt again!"

"Don't worry Laura, I have a good feeling about this."

"It's a shame about her daughter, isn't it Dad? Losing her partner."

"Yeah it is, Laura."

"I was thinking Dad, if he died last week, what was it that made her daughter call her mum when you had a date

93

with her yesterday? As she should of been more OK about it by then."

"Maybe she is totally distraught with it all and maybe with the funeral being today she just got anxious I guess Laura."

"Yeah, I guess so Dad, just something you wouldn't normally do, but I guess the poor girl must be really down."

"Well, she is seeing me again tomorrow so that's all right by me!"

"OK Dad, but be careful and take your time with her."

"Hey! Am the parent!" he replied,

Laura laughed and said, "You're like a big soft kid at times!" and she was right.

Shaun played with his grandson for a while longer then headed off home and as he drove he thought about the comment from his own daughter about the phone call that made Kath leave him to see her distraught daughter, *'hmm, maybe she had a point there, ohh, I don't know'.*

The rest of the day took an age to pass and all he could think about was Kath, he noticed that that anxious feeling was starting to come back and he plonked himself down on the sofa and lost himself in his thoughts. He kept thinking about his new start in life with the money and all the little things he wanted to do and one of them was hopefully meet someone again that he could care for and love. He sat there and came to the conclusion that as long as he was bloody careful with the money then no one needed to know and, yes, it was only early days with Kath but something just seemed so right between them, *'but how can I look at her daughter,'* he thought, *'knowing I seen him dead and took the money for myself?'* A brew was needed, and a cig, somehow he kept his mind on the fact that he wanted a new start in life and since he had found the bag he actually felt he was living a life rather than going through the motions like he was before he found the bag and, although he still felt anxious, he found not only the strength but the need to see it through. With his fresh brew made, he headed off to the garden for a cig and enjoyed the moment, not the moment of having a cig but the moment of knowing there was no going back.

As the night came around he waited for Kath to call and eventually it happened, "Hi Kath, how are you?"

She explained how tough a day it was, seeing her daughter upset like that, and then from nowhere she asked him to come around and see her tonight, "I really need someone to talk too," she explained.

Shaun replied, "I would love to."

Kath gave him her address and he wrote it down and said, "I can see you in an hour?"

"Yeah, that's great Shaun, see you then."

He quickly ran upstairs, had a very quick shower and threw some clean clothes on. He typed her address into his sat nav, he knew the area as it wasn't too far from the West Derby area he lived in, but he just didn't know the avenue she lived in. He put a quick splash of aftershave on, a squirt of Lynx and a brush of his teeth and he was ready, his heart was beating like a drum with excitement as he fired up the car.

Within minutes he was driving up the avenue she lived in and parked up the car just outside her house. It was a really nice house which was set just off the road and her front garden looked fantastic and well cared for. As he got out of the car and walked towards the door Kath came out and invited him inside. She took him into the lounge and, just as the house looked beautiful from the outside, it did on the inside too, "Lovely place you have, Kath."

"Yeah, it is. I love my home but damn hard to keep on top of it though."

"I can imagine, Kath; my house is so tiny compared to this but trying to keep it tidy is a full-time job."

"Would you like a tea or coffee Shaun?"

"Yeah, tea please, 1 sugar."

As she walked into the kitchen he followed her and she took his hands and said, "I am so glad you could come up."

He let go of her hands, placed his arms around her and pulled her towards him and he held her tight in his arms. She lifted her head up from his shoulder and he gently kissed her soft lips, she then pressed her lips harder against his and let out a small moan, she pulled away from his lips and said, "I think we better take our tea inside, otherwise we may be here all night!"

Shaun wouldn't have minded that at all but agreed, "Yeah, come on, let's get inside."

They sat on the sofa and she told him how the funeral went and how she had left the reception afterwards as she didn't like the vibes that had surrounded her.

"What was wrong, Kath? Why would there be bad vibes?"

"Oh, there was a few unwanted faces at the funeral," she explained, "not good people am afraid."

"Oh, if you don't mind me saying, Kath, I thought he was a policeman and guessed all his friends would be good people?"

Kath shook her head and said, "No, not this policeman, Shaun. I knew he was trouble from the first time my daughter brought him 'round to see me, he just had that shifty look and made me feel uncomfortable with all his boasting about some of the crimes he was involved in. I think my daughter was foolish to get involved with him, but he showered her with expensive gifts and not just for her but for my grandkids too."

"Oh, so the kids aren't his?"

"Oh no, they're from another relationship that went pear shaped."

Shaun was now getting more curious about the funeral, "So was there a lot from the police force there then?"

"There was a few but we thought it was best to keep it more low key, there was also a few who wanted to speak to my daughter at the end of it too."

"Talk to her, Kath?"

"Yeah, they wanted to interview her on some questions again and, rather than tell them to come 'round another time, she answered there questions then."

"Bloody hell, the man had only just been buried!"

"To be truthful, Shaun, they have had my daughter in a few times for questioning since his death."

"Oh right, err, why would that be Kath?"

"They think she may have knew why he was there that night he was shot and also did she know anything about what he was doing in the days leading up to the shooting. You see Shaun, and please don't tell anyone, but he wasn't officially on duty that night and the police are trying to play it down as they don't want to draw attention to what has happened, especially with the success of the jewel heist robbery, and I guess as a dead men cannot talk the police are trying to keep this under wraps. But it seems he was a bad copper and was trying to make some money for himself."

"Bloody hell, Kath, sounds a nightmare this guy, in fact, the whole bloody thing!"

"It is, Shaun, and I don't think it's over for my daughter."

Shaun's mind was now running in overdrive but tried to keep a calm outlook. He said, "Why don't you think it's over for your daughter, Kath?"

She looked at Shaun and shook her head and replied, "Beth is acting very strange of late."

"In what way strange Kath? As she is probably just shocked by his death."

"Yeah, she was, but when she called me and I left you to get to her it seemed like something else had spooked her, she wouldn't tell me what, but I could see she was scared."

"Sounds to me, Kath, you need to have a good heart to heart with her when the time is right."

"Am really sorry, Shaun, you must think terrible of us."

"Hey, Kath, it's OK, it's not your fault, any of this. How many times when you was younger did you follow the wrong path? And that's all Beth has done and I'm sure now she will stop and turn around and walk down the right path from now on, she simply got caught up with the wrong guy and she will get over it and move on and hopefully learn."

"You're a good man, Shaun, and I hope you're right and I pray that Beth will take the right path and meet someone who is good next time."

Shaun put his arms around her and held her close, "How about another cup of tea, eh, Kath?"

"Good idea," she said, gave him a smile and headed off to the kitchen, and you could see she was putting a brave face on.

He sat back on the sofa and thought of all the things she had told him, then Kath's voice shouted over, "Would you like a sandwich or a biscuit?"

"Ohh, big decision that, Kath. But yeah, go on. Biscuits for me, please," he said cheerfully, trying to raise her spirits as it was clear she was really upset with the whole ordeal of it. "So, where are the grandkids Kath?"

"Oh, they're fast asleep upstairs, they're in bed by 7:30 every night when they're with me. I put them to bed and tell them a story and normally most nights there asleep within minutes."

"Oh, so your daughter doesn't live with you then?"

"No, but she doesn't live that far from here, she left home just over 3 years ago, though I haven't a clue why as she is in here most nights with me. I think the main reason she left was she wanted her own space, especially when having the 2nd child, plus me and my husband wasn't getting on at the time and it wasn't a nice place to be in, and just as she left my husband walked out 2 months later."

"Oh, am sorry to hear that, Kath."

"It's OK Shaun, we was over 2 years prior to that, in truth, when I found out he was having an affair."

"Oh, that normally does it," he replied.

"Yeah, it does," she said, "I tried to put it behind me and we tried to move forward together, but he never stopped seeing her and he left me to go and live with that woman, the nights I spent wondering what I had done wrong and why he didn't want me anymore and what could I have done better to keep him seemed endless when we split up. Then eventually I realised that it was simply down to him and nothing I could have done would have changed it. The way I see it now is she can have him as he isn't worth it."

"You're right there, Kath, as these things just happen, no matter what you do and you cannot blame yourself."

"Yeah, I know, Shaun. But I am over it now and, like I said, it was over a long time before the split as we simply stopped loving each other but I did feel betrayed and that's why I haven't till now looked for anyone else. I just got stuck into my work and looking after my grandkids more and got on with my life. I actually enjoyed being single," and then with a big smile she said, "till you came along and drugged my coffee."

"Ha-ha, well, it simply had to be done, Kath."

"You make me smile, Shaun, and not just on the outside but in the inside too. Even today at the funeral my thoughts was drifting back to us in the coffee shop for the 1st time

100

and me taking you, who at the time was a total stranger, to the shoe shop. I couldn't help but laugh when you took out a pen and scribbled your number on a receipt as you looked a bundle of nerves."

"I was nervous, Kath, and I wanted to shout out to you as you walked away from the coffee shop, but luckily you turned 'round."

"Am glad I did, Shaun."

Shaun reached over and kissed her gently. As the kisses became more intense and passionate her phone started to ring, "I better get that," she said.

"Hi Beth, you OK?" she said then listened carefully to the call and said, "OK then, cya soon," and hung up.

She turned back to Shaun, "That was Beth, she is coming back to stay with me tonight as she doesn't want to be on her own this evening."

"I understand, Kath."

"It's a shame," she replied, "as I was enjoying them kisses."

"Me too," he jokingly replied, "listen, maybe it's best that I get off home before Beth gets here, as the last thing she would want to see is me as she needs you tonight."

"OK, Shaun, it's been lovely. Thank you for coming over and sorry I keep on cutting us short."

He smiled, kissed her gently once more and headed for the car, "Cya soon baby, hope Beth is OK."

He gave a quick wave, powered up the car and drove away.

He decided to stop off at Maccies on the way home and grab a latte and he sat in his car having a cig and drinking his latte and re-living the night in his mind, especially her kisses which seemed so gentle yet so sexy, and how he tried his best to control himself as it had been a while but somehow he did, courtesy of the phone call from her daughter. He felt so good and sat in the car park for a good 30 minutes before setting off home.

On getting home Barney was sniffing around him, "Yes, Barney, your Dad has been with another woman," Barney instantly sat by the door and Shaun knew what that meant, "OK lad, where is your lead?"

Barney raced over to the chair where the lead was and off they walked through the estate. Shaun was on cloud nine and nothing in the world was going to change this tonight.

On getting back home he had a glass of juice and give Barney a little bite to eat and reflected on his day again. Then he started to think about the money and the diamonds again, *'geez, what a week this has been,'* he thought. He was really starting to believe that he had kicked off the shackles of his shambolic marriage and all the hurt and pain he endured and the lonely nights of wondering how it went wrong and where does he go from here, but here and now he was alive and kicking and ready for a new beginning, He switched on the TV and watched the end of a movie and, as he was watching, his eyes were starting to close. He locked the house up and went to bed and fell asleep the minute his head hit the pillow.

18th April

His eyes opened and reached over to his phone it was 7am and the alarm was banging away. If it didn't go off, God knows what time he would have woken up this morning as he was in such a deep sleep. Sitting on the edge of the bed he rubbed his eyes and said, "God, am knackered," and headed off to the bathroom to throw some water on his face.

The 3 S's could wait this morning as he went down the stairs and put the kettle on. Throwing his house coat on, he let Barney into the garden and headed back in to make his brew. His thoughts were still with Kath, and as he thought of her, his face gave birth to the 1st smile of the day. Grabbing his tea, he ventured into the garden and sat on the bench, lit up a roll up, checked his phone for the latest news and sport and read intensely the news of a possible new Liverpool FC new signing, he hoped he would be the one to fire them to glory this year. With his brew and cig finished he went back inside and the 3 S's began.

After that, he threw some clothes on and took Barney out for a morning walk. It wasn't a great morning but spring was certainly trying to push through as it felt slightly warmer this morning. On his way back home his text alert went off on his phone, it was Kath and it simply said: *"Morning Sexy Man! how are you today? X."* As soon as he got home he text back and said: *"Hey Sexy Lady. am good thanks and how's you? x."* His phone then rang.

"Hiya Shaun, am glad you're up as I couldn't wait to talk to you again."

"That's nice Kath, as you have been on my mind since I woke up too."

"Am just getting breakfast ready for the grandkids as they will be out of bed soon."

"How's Beth today, Kath?"

"Well, we sat and talked for a while, but I don't think she is telling me everything, though I did mention you to her and she is happy for me."

"That's nice, Kath, am sure things will be fine in time with her."

"I hope so," she replied, "is it OK if I call you later on, Shaun?"

"Hey! You can call me anytime you want to lovely, am only doing my chores today and a bit of shopping."

"Great then," she said, "I will call you later, and till then, mwah."

Shaun blew a kiss back and headed off to the kitchen to fix Barney up some food and then jumped into his car and headed off to Sainsbury's. Rather than do his shopping first he headed to the cafe inside the store and got a bacon bap and a latte. He glanced at a morning paper that someone had left on the table as he devoured his bacon bap and he noticed a small article on the burial of the policeman, it was only a small column with the last part saying only family and close friends attended as they wanted a low-key affair. His thoughts then centred back on reality as, up until then, his head has been up in the clouds being all loved up. Sipping at his latte he then thought about

Kath saying that her daughter's partner was trouble and not to be trusted and that Beth had been questioned herself a few times, Shaun's mind went into overdrive as he tried piecing things together, *'hmm, maybe her daughter does know a lot more than what she is telling,'* and with that a new thought came into his mind, *'what if the police are watching her! As if they're watching her, then they will be watching her mum and that means they will be wondering who the hell I am! Some new man walking into her mum's house, geez, that's not the plan that'.* He quickly drank up his latte and walked around the aisles, picking up what he needed. He left the store in a hurry, loaded up the car and headed straight home.

Putting all the stuff he bought away, he made a brew, rolled up a cig and sat in the garden once more. He thought about the scenario of the police making enquiries about him as it was more than likely that they were interested in Kath's daughter, *'and if they are watching her and ask who on earth is this chap with the mother and then come around to speak to me and, God forbid, have a search warrant, then that's game over man'.* He then thought of the scenario of trying to explain to the police that he found the bag and out of sheer luck he met the mother of the daughter in a coffee shop in town, *'they simply wouldn't believe it and lock me up and throw away the bloody key, geez, maybe I should hide the money and the diamonds better, but then again the police are experts at looking in all the places you think they wouldn't look so I may as well just leave them where they are, but I got to do something'.* He went back into the house and gave it more thought, *'maybe am overthinking this, maybe they was just asking questions in case she knew anything of her partner rather than her being caught up in it, as for the life in me I cannot see her being involved in all this as they would have locked her up by now'.* Once again his mind was racing but appeared to be making some sense of it all, he always had a good mind for working things out and this week he has been tested to the full but all that matters is that he wasn't caught with the bag and now he has to be even more careful, the only way he could understand it a bit more was if he asked Kath some more questions.

The morning had flew by and he was starting to get hungry again and made himself a few ham butties and a brew. As he was just finishing them he got a text from Kath: ***"Can I call you Shaun if you're not busy?"*** and taking a big swig of tea to wash the last of the butty down he punched in the reply of: "***Yes, that's great."*** His phone rang within seconds of sending the text.

"Hiya, Kath. you OK"

"Yeah, am good thanks, Shaun. My daughter has just taken the grandkids home and I wondered whether you fancy a coffee in the cafe by Alderhey hospital, you know, the one on the corner called Claire's."

"Yeah, I know it well, Kath. What time you want to meet?"

"Say about 15 mins?"

"Okey dokey, Kath, catch you then."

Shaun quickly freshened up his face, threw some aftershave on and drove up towards the cafe. Trying to find a parking space here was the hardest thing of all but luckily today a space appeared and, quick as a flash, he parked up in it. He ordered 2 Lattes and sat outside in the tabled area and waited for Kath. Out of nowhere she appeared and waved from the other side of the road. Shaun stood up and kissed her on the cheek.

"Oh good, you got the coffees in then."

"Yes, I've already put some drugs in yours to keep you liking me."

She gave out a big laugh and sat down, "I think them drugs are irreversible," she said and she reached out and held his hand.

"I hope so," said Shaun, "as I could get used to looking at that lovely face of yours."

"Oh, I don't know," she said, "you must think am crazy texting you and calling you and wanting to see you every day, you will probably get fed up with me."

Shaun could see she was feeling vulnerable with meeting someone new. He looked at into Kath's eyes and said, "Hey you, am just like you too, I feel the same and the only reason I didn't ask to see you first last night was simply that I thought you wouldn't have wanted to see me after the funeral, otherwise I would have asked to see you too. So don't stop being you, and don't stop asking to see me as I want to see you just as much."

"I just feel I have blabbed on and on about me and my daughter and haven't given you a chance, Shaun."

"Well, I tell you what Kath, let's jump in the cars and go to Croxteth park and have a stroll around the park and I will tell you all about me, and if you try to interrupt me, I will just have to kiss you each time you do."

"That sounds like a good idea Shaun, let's go."

They finished their coffees, got into their cars and drove to the park.

On parking up, they held each other's hands and strolled through this beautiful park, "It's crazy, Shaun, that every time I have you to myself my daughter calls me."

"Well, I hope you left the phone in the car," said Shaun and they both laughed.

Kath explained why she loved Croxteth park so much and how as a child she always wanted to live in the mansion that's right in the middle of the park.

Shaun laughed and said, "Hey! I would buy it for you if I won the lottery."

The one thing Shaun loved about this park was that it had so much to offer in way of paths leading to all sorts of places and even a farm, but there was one place he did love which was just by the small lake. Just as they got close to the mansion there was an ice cream van and he bought 2 big ice creams with all the trimmings on and headed for his favourite place. He parked himself down on the bench and, as they both got stuck in to the ice creams, he spoke of his own life to Kath.

After he had spoken for a while Kath looked at Shaun and said, "You're still angry with her, aren't you?"

"I am angry, as I know I was stupid to marry her as all the warning signs was there beforehand."

"Well at least you are away from that life now Shaun and I know there is always 2 sides of a story but you couldn't live your life under them conditions, seems like her eldest daughter had a problem with the world."

"You're telling me, Kath, she was an adult with a child's mind, but it was up to her mum to stop it but I guess she had her own problems and coupled with her daughter's, and then mine, the inevitable happened. But it's for the best as it was a horrible time in my life, Kath. I thought it was going to scar me forever and then one day I went for a cup of coffee and…!"

Kath burst in then by saying, "Ha-ha, yes, you drugged my coffee, Shaun."

They sat by lake and chatted for ages and he spoke to her of his first marriage and his own children who are now all grown up.

"It's nice that you still get on well with your 1st wife, Shaun."

"Yeah, she is a good woman, and a great mum to our children."

He spoke of his days in rock bands and all the weekends with his children and how he basically has been stumbling through life till present day.

"You have done so much with your life, Shaun, you're very lucky to have experienced all the things you have."

"Yeah, it comes at a cost though, but I am very lucky to have 3 great kids and had some great times with the bands, met some wonderful people along the way, but it was always about the music with me rather than the band scene. I just loved the thrill of playing live and people enjoying the songs we as a band wrote."

"Tell me more about your children?" Kath asked.

Shaun spoke of his 2 daughters and son, about watching them grow and how every weekend they would come to stay with him and the fun they had had, and one day in particular when he was chasing them with a cup of water to throw over them and as he came down the stairs his eldest daughter threw a whole basin of water all over him, drowning him and soaking all the carpet and stairs.

"It doesn't sound that funny, Kath, but if you would have seen it, as she was hid behind the door for ages and took me totally by surprise! In a way, we was all like kids together and I was the big kid. We had some good times together like that and now that they have all grown up and got their own lives I miss all that fun when they was kids, especially the stories I told them all of a night. But now they made me a grandad and I have a grandson and granddaughter now."

"So, what did your kids think about your 2nd wife?"

"They wasn't that keen on the family but put up with it for me, I guess. They're glad am away from all that now as they knew how unhappy I was with them."

"I wonder what they will think of me," Kath said.

"Well, they're good judges, my kids, so am sure they will love you. It's funny though, Kath, a few weeks ago I was still struggling with everything in my life and then like a switch it just clicked and I felt free and at ease with myself, and then the last week has been like a rollercoaster of a ride and I love the feeling of being me again."

Shaun knew he nearly tripped himself up as he was referring to finding the bag as the rollercoaster ride, "With meeting you, Kath, and some stuff at work it's been a great week."

"It's been a rollercoaster ride for me too, Shaun, with my daughter's partner getting killed and all the upset of it all, and then in the middle of it I found you, it's crazy the way life works, isn't it?"

"You better believe it," Shaun replied, "life has a canny habit of throwing all different permutations up and bringing people together."

Kath replied by saying, "I think its fate, and people are brought together for a reason."

Shaun thought to himself, *'if only you knew how right you were, Kath!'* There was a slight lull in the conversation as Shaun looked around the area and then told Kath why this bench was so special to him, as for nearly 10 years he had not only brought his kids to this spot but also his mum and had they sat on the bench looking at the views whilst having a small picnic. The bench was right next to a small lake that was normally covered in a dark green moss, he could see in his mind his son trying to climb every tree in sight and his 2 daughters looking over the iron fencing at the little lake, waiting for air bubbles to pop up so they could say they had seen a fish, and then he told her of his mum who loved the park and would love nothing better than to sit on the bench and have a cup of tea from a flask and enjoy a cigarette, "She would chat about all things from when she was younger and how she loved feeding the ducks, my mum loved nature. One day, when it was just me and my mum at the park, we came across a small bridge that crossed a stream which is just a bit further up from here and, maybe it was the dementia kicking in, but when she looked over the bridge she thought it was a wishing well and I gave her a coin to throw in. I asked her what her wish was but she smiled and said "no, it won't come true if I tell you." I miss her smiles."

Kath looked at Shaun and said, "You done a great job of looking after your mum for all them years, she was lucky to have you."

Shaun smiled and replied, "Quite the opposite as I think I was lucky to have her, she made me realise how, even in the most difficult circumstances, to look for the good and find a smile and see beauty in the things around us."

They got off the bench and walked through the park and Kath stopped by a huge tree and said, "You can kiss me if you want."

Shaun grinned, "Err, yeah, OK."

She gave him a look to say 'get yourself over here'. He held her in his arms and pressed against her as she leaned back against the tree and they kissed passionately.

"We are like two kids, kissing in the park," said Kath, "but, God, that was nice."

"Someone once said to me, Kath, that nice is a cup of tea!"

"Ha-ha, yeah, you're right there, Shaun. Then I would have to say that was amazing, is that better?"

"Well, besides the drugs business am also in the amazing business too."

She laughed and said, "In your dreams. Come on, let's get back, eh. Oh, there is one more thing I want to ask you Shaun. I haven't got the grandkids round tonight and am wondering if you would like to come over and see me tonight."

"Sounds like a good plan to me, Kath."

They held each other's hand till they got back to the cars and kissed each other once more and they both headed home. Shaun's mind was already in overdrive as he felt this was going to be a good night!

On getting home he quickly sent Kath a text and said: *"Soz babe but what time tonight?"* His reply was instant: *"8ish x."*

He then took Barney for a quick walk and, on getting back, he made another couple of sandwiches and a brew and, as normal, both him and Barney ate the butties. After finishing his brew he went out to the garden, lit up a cig and thought about his wonderful day in the park with Kath, *'I know she jokes with me about me drugging her coffee but I feel totally mesmerised by her charm and beauty, it's like I am drugged too'.*

After his cig he opted for a quick shower again and once more let the warm water run down his face as he thought about the day and night ahead of him. After getting dried he hit the new deodorant and splashed some of his favourite aftershave, Kokorico. Some clean clothes and he was ready, but he still had 2 hours to go, so he opted for a quick drive to Maccies for a coke and some chicken nuggets just to kill some time as he was far too excited to be hanging around the house.

He still had just over an hour to go so he picked up the Liverpool Echo and read through it, there was a bigger article about the dead policeman's funeral and he lit up a cig and got his mind to work on what he read. Time still appeared to be dragging and he sent a text asking Kath if she wanted anything from the shop. Her reply was she didn't need anything but to get his arse over to hers now, to which he fired up the car and drove straight to hers. He didn't need to set the sat nav as he knew his way this time and drove as fast as he could to get there.

He pulled in to the driveway, got out and rang the bell. She popped her head around the door and invited him in. As he stepped inside she took his hand and guided him up the stairs to her bedroom.

She undid her robe which fell to the floor and said, "Now, where were we under that tree?"

Shaun's eyes opened wide and he pulled her towards him and held her tightly. He kissed her soft lips and neck and lost himself in the moment of passion and desire. Every touch and taste was like a new experience as she guided him to the bed and undressed him. It had been a while for both since they shared this intimacy with someone, and tonight they made love with a heightened desire and want.

They lay in each other's arms and even then, Shaun felt her body fitted him perfectly. He looked at Kath and said, "Well, I wasn't expecting that!"

"Oh yes, you was, but maybe not quite like that," she replied.

He smiled and said, "Well, err, I guess so. The robe thing was just pure class, you're adorable Kath."

The 2 of them kissed some more and made love again.

After making love again Shaun lay there, pleasantly exhausted, as Kath went to grab a quick shower. He knew his 54-year-old body had just had a good work out and, judging by the way his body felt, he knew he had better get in shape for the future. Kath shouted out to Shaun that she had finished her shower if he fancied a shower too.

"Yeah, fantastic babe. I will be out now if I can manage to get out of the bed," he laughed.

Kath shouted back, "And here was me being easy on you too!"

He got out of the bed, kissed Kath on the neck and went for his shower. The adrenaline and amazement of making love filled his body as the hot water eased his tense muscles. As he got out and dried himself, he sat on the edge of the bath and thought about how lucky he was to have met Kath and just how special she makes him feel.

He walked down the stairs and she placed a big mug of tea in front of him, "You earned that," she said jokingly.

"I would have hoped I earned a biscuit or two as well!"

"Hmm, yeah, I guess so," she said.

They both flopped on the sofa and Kath mentioned that she was having the grandkids around tomorrow with her daughter and did he fancy coming around for dinner!

He looked at Kath and said, "This reminds me of when I was a lad and I would bring my girl 'round to meet my mother!"

They both laughed and she said, "You're probably right there, as I would like you to meet my daughter."

"Yeah, I would love to meet them, Kath."

Kath then mentioned a great series on the TV that she had been watching called 'Banshee'.

"Hey, I've been watching that too, Kath, and I've watched the first series, let's get it on now as I haven't seen the second series yet."

She looked at Shaun and said, "Hmm, that's nice, we even share the same taste in tele."

The night was simply fantastic as they both sat back and watched an episode of Banshee.

Afterwards, they went into the garden, lit up a cig each and chatted away further. Then Shaun gave Kath another kiss and said, "Listen, babe, it's getting a bit late now, so am going to get off home and let you have a good night's sleep. What time shall I come 'round tomorrow?"

"Err, how about 2 o'clock, Shaun."

"Yep, that's great babe."

As she opened the front door Shaun pulled her close to him and kissed her one more time and said his goodbyes and waved as he walked down the path.

Shaun felt amazing on the drive home and as soon as he got home he clipped the lead on Barney and took him out for a short walk. The night sky looked somehow even more beautiful than normal and he and Barney strolled along the dimly lit streets without a care in the world.

On getting back he brewed up and walked into the garden, lit up a cig and enjoyed the moments of the evening in his mind. The loneliness and despair and frustration that he had endured so much in the last year had simply vanished in the last 8 days, and excitement and prosperity coupled with anxiety and fear and now love has risen in the strangest of circumstances and he knew his life was never

116

going to be the same again. Shaun's thoughts then turned to meeting her daughter and how he is going to deal with the fact he had seen her partner and took the bag from him, but for now those thoughts could wait.

He went back into the house and locked up and went to bed a happy man. He slept like log that night and even if a brass band was playing in the next room, he would not have woken up.

19th April

His eyes slowly opened as he reached for his phone and couldn't believe his eyes to see it was 08:30 as it was always like clockwork that he opened his eyes just before the phone alarm went off at 7am! He got out of bed, he ached in parts he hadn't ached in for a while due to the workout he got last night, and headed straight to the bathroom, right into the shower and let the hot water ease his aching back and legs. He stayed in the shower longer than normal as he reflected once more on last night. With all bathroom duties now complete he got changed and went downstairs to be greeted by Barney and let him out into the garden. Brew made, he went into the garden, sat on the bench and called Barney over to him. As he patted Barney on the head he said, "Thanks, mate, for your help in finding me the bag and Kath."

Barney just looked at him, not having a clue what he was saying to him, but wagged his tail anyways and ran to the gate waiting to be taken out for his morning walk. But he could wait a while longer this morning as Shaun's brew was only half drunk and his first cig of the day was born. His mind focused on Kath's daughter and he knew how difficult it was going to be seeing her, not just for the first time but for as long as his relationship with Kath lasted, and that would hopefully be a very long time. A part of him knew he couldn't carry that with him forever but he had to as he didn't want to go back in life - only forward. *'Let's see how it goes,'* he thought to himself and then got up and took Barney out for his walk.

The walk this morning was like most mornings, his mind deep in thoughts about the contents of the bag, thoughts that filled him with anxiety and fear, and even though he had one of the best evenings for a long time last night he could feel the anxiety starting to creep back in as he thought more about Kath's daughter and her dead partner and the contents of the bag.

On getting home he went into the garden and tended to his plants and let his thoughts roll around in his head.

An hour later he made some breakfast and as he ate it he felt the anxiousness come creeping back over him, "For Christ's sake, what's wrong with me?" he asked loudly.

He walked back into the garden and decided to call his own daughter. She was delighted to hear from him and he told her all about yesterday and how great things were with Kath, minus certain details, and told her about lunch today with Kath.

"Ahh, Dad, am so happy for you! She sounds perfect for you, you will have to call me tonight and let me know how lunch went today."

"I will Laura."

After he finished talking to Laura he called his other daughter, Claire, and let her know how he was doing. Like Laura, she was happy for him,

"Go for it dad but just don't dive in," she said, "just go with it slowly."

'Too late,' thought Shaun as not only has he dived in but he has also done a triple somersault on the way down.

Shaun's son would still be in bed as he didn't come alive till 3 in the afternoon, as most 21-year-old lads do after a Saturday night on the town, so it would be a waste of time calling him. However, he did feel good about telling his daughters that he was doing well and they were happy for him as they hated the fact he may be struggling on his own after all the crap he has had to deal with the last few years with the ex.

A few brews later he got a text from Kath telling him to come around any time after 1 o'clock he replied saying that was great and he couldn't wait. He took himself upstairs, went into the loft and sat there looking at the money and the diamonds and stared at the gun, *'I wonder how this thing works,'* he thought. With that, he took the name of the gun and went downstairs on to his computer, hit the name of the gun into the search bar and watched the results for Glock 19 handgun come up, *'geez, there is so much info here,'* he thought and spent time looking at YouTube to see how you fire the thing and what it is capable of, *'geez, this is some weapon,'* he thought.

The time drew close to one o'clock and he got himself ready and fired up the car and went round to Kath's, if finding the bag and what has happened next made him tense, then this was up there with it too, as when he pulled up outside Kath's house he could feel a tension building up in his back and neck.

She came out to meet him on the path, "Hello you," she said and gave him a quick kiss on the cheek and they walked in together, "Beth isn't here yet, she will be here about 2 o'clock, I guess I just wanted you to myself for an hour before she gets here."

"That's nice, Kath."

"Come on," she said, "let's sit outside in the garden and have a cup of tea, or would you like a coffee, it's filter coffee!"

"Yeah, filter coffee sounds great, Kath."

She brought the coffee out into the garden and they sat there chatting about last night.

"If you don't mind me saying, Shaun, but are you OK? You seem a little distant."

"Oh, am sorry, Kath. It may sound crazy but I feel a bit nervous with meeting your daughter, Beth."

"There's no need for you to be nervous, Shaun."

"I think, with all the trouble I had with the ex-wife's daughter, it seems really important that I make a favourable impression."

"You will, Shaun, don't worry, honey. If I like you, which I do, then that will be good enough for her too. I don't let my kids run my life, I like to think we respect each other as equals and enjoy each other's lives, rather than interfere and dictate, she is a big softy really."

"I hope so," he replied.

They lit a cig and discussed the Sunday roast they was going to have later, "I can cook a good lamb or beef joint," he said and went into chef mode, clearly trying to impress Kath.

"Well, one day I will put that to the test," she said, "I hope you didn't think I was too forward last night, Shaun. I just wanted you to know how much I wanted you…"

Before she could say anything else, Shaun stood up, took her hand and pulled her towards him. He kissed her strongly and whispered in her ear that if her daughter wasn't coming around shortly, then he would show her how much he wanted her too right now.

"I guess the drugs you put in my coffee still influenced me last night," she said.

"Well, I better put some more in later then," he replied, "as I like the way you think and, like you, I also like you a lot, Kath, you make me feel great."

They went to kiss again but were interrupted by the sound of the doorbell. Shaun's heart started to pump faster as Kath said, "This must be her now."

He could tell by the commotion outside that the kids were in full hyper mode too.

"Nanny!" they shouted, as they ran into the house.

Turning himself around to view down the hall he noticed a black BMW 5 series parked outside, *'nice car,'* he thought, *'she is obviously doing well'*.

Kath brought Beth outside to see him, "Beth, this is Shaun, Shaun this is Beth."

He smiled and said hello to Beth. She said hello back and then turned around to sort the kids out. Even in that split second of eye contact he could see that she was either upset or anxious, "Hey, great kids, Beth, are they good?"

She replied by saying that they would test the patience of a saint. Kath quickly intervened by saying, "They're lovely kids for their Nanny, aren't you, boys?"

The 2 boys nodded their heads as they looked at Shaun.

"Hey, what a cool car you have," said Shaun to the eldest boy as he was holding a toy car, "let's see it then, does it go fast?"

Barry showed Shaun the car and you could instantly see that he had a new mate as he told Shaun that its much faster than his brother's fire engine. The younger boy, Carl, looked on and held his mother's hand, but it wasn't long before Shaun was entertaining the 2 lads with some magic tricks he used to do with his own children when they were young like the vanishing pound trick, which often kept his kids amused for ages, and did exactly the same with these 2 little boys. Kath was really happy and you could see it in her face as she got the dinner ready.

"Dinner's ready now," she shouted, "so all sit 'round the table, boys."

Shaun couldn't help but notice how well behaved the boys were and they sat at the table as they were told. Kath put the dinner down on the table and it looked good, but he couldn't help but notice that Beth didn't seem that happy at all, her face looked strained, almost tired looking. He looked at Beth again and asked her if she was OK.

"Not really," she said, "just seems to be one thing after another of late."

"I can imagine," he said.

She looked right into Shaun's eyes and said, "I doubt you could imagine, but thanks anyways."

He could see in her face a touch of vulnerability and he noticed her eyes glistening up. He put his head down and looked at his dinner and felt totally uncomfortable with the situation as all his senses were telling him that something was very wrong. Yeah, it could be that she is still in mourning over her loss, but her voice in the way she said 'I doubt you would understand', told him that something else wasn't right.

Kath tried to change the mood of the table and told the boys that if they eat all their carrots and peas, then they would grow up big, strong, boys. The dinner itself was as good as it looked and the roast spuds and the home-made Yorkshire pudding was to die for. Beth said a few things to her mum and Kath looked over at Shaun and gave an expression with her face showing sympathy to Beth.

They sat there and ate their dinners and he passed his compliments to the chef. They chatted somewhat as they ate, but the atmosphere just didn't seem quite right. After they had eaten he volunteered to take out all the plates.

"Just leave them in the sink," Kath shouted, "I will sort them later."

"Will do, Kath."

He stood there by the sink, knowing this was not such a good idea after all, as the last thing Beth wanted right now was to see her mum with another man so soon after her losing her man.

Kath came out into the kitchen too and asked him if he was OK.

"Yeah, I'm OK, babe, I just think Beth isn't ready for this just yet."

"Hmm, you may be right Shaun."

"Listen Kath, I will go back inside and carry on my magic tricks with the lads for a short while, and then I will get off to let you and Beth talk about things."

She smiled and said, "OK then, at least she has seen you," and she kissed him on the cheek.

Shaun went outside for a quick cig before he returned to the room and, as he lit up his cig, Beth came out too as she enjoyed an occasional cigarette.

As she lit her cig she said, "Listen, Shaun, am sorry if I have come across as being rude, but my head is up my own arse at the moment and I didn't mean anything by it, but I really need to talk to Mum."

"Hey, you're OK, Beth," he had to stop himself from saying I understand as, quite clearly, he didn't, "am off home in about 10 minutes Beth, and it's been great meeting you and the boys and hope we can do it again sometime."

"Yes, that would be nice, Shaun."

Walking back inside he spoke to Kath and told her that Beth needed to speak to her and, after doing a bit more magic for the boys, he said his goodbyes and headed for the car.

Kath walked down the path to him and thanked him once more for coming and she seemed slightly upset that he was going but it was clearly the right thing to do, "Thanks for that lovely dinner Kath, cya soon lovely, and call me when you get a chance this evening."

The 2 lads came running out and he performed one more last trick, making sure they won the pound this time, and waved goodbye. He fired up the car and normally he would put the radio on, but he sat there in silence as he drove away. He knew this was too soon to see Beth, but at the same time he knew it would be foolish if he thought it was going to be easy with the present situation, and kicked himself for being so wrapped up in his own world that he didn't consider how Beth would be feeling.

The next few hours passed and he got some clothes ready for work for the next day and checked his phone for messages, but alas none.

It was now nearly 8pm and he took his favourite position out in the garden with a fresh brew and lit up a cig. As he lit up the cig his phone rang, it was Kath.

He tried to sound cheerful, "Hey, hello you, I've missed you and its only been a few hours!"

Nothing but silence came back. "Hey, you OK, Kath? Kath?! You there?"

He could hear crying in the background, "Hey Kath, please talk to me, are you OK, love?"

"Shaun it's terrible!"

"What is Kath?"

"It's so terrible," she replied again.

"Kath, talk to me, please! What's wrong, Kath?

"Can I come over to you? Shaun, I will tell you all then."

"Please do, Kath. You know how to get here?"

"Yes, I will find it, cya soon then."

"Kath…" the phone just cut off.

'Bloody hell, I wonder what's gone on here!' he thought and then set about the house like a mad man, trying to tidy it up before she arrived. He splashed some aftershave on, brewed up and lit up another cig outside whilst he waited. Then he heard the car pull up outside and

he went out to greet her, all her body language suggested something very bad has happened. He sat her down in the garden and she went into her bag and pulled out a cig, he noticed her hands shaking.

"What's up, baby? What's happened?"

She looked up at him, her eyes were all puffed up and she put her arms around him and started crying on his shoulder, her whole body was juddering as she sobbed so heavily.

"Hey, baby, please tell me what's wrong!"

"They're going to kill her, Shaun!"

"Eh?! What do you mean, Kath?"

"They're going to kill her!"

"Who is going to kill her and kill who?"

"They're going to kill Beth, Shaun."

"Sorry, honey, but why would anyone want to kill Beth?"

"They think she is involved with her partner, and, err, well it appears she was, Shaun!"

"What, the shooting, Kath?"

"No, Shaun, the whole bloody thing!"

"But, err, am struggling with this, Kath, please tell me it all. How did this come about and who is going to kill her?"

He gave her some tissues to wipe away the tears and blow her nose, she looked up at him and said, "Am sorry for bringing this your way but I have no one else to turn to."

"Hey, am glad, am here for you, babe, don't be sorry at all. Just tell me what's wrong and how it's all came about."

"It was just after you left today, Shaun. Beth apologised to me for being rude to you and told me she would explain when she got the kids to sleep later, and after she put them to bed she came down and sat me on the sofa and told me it all. That night of the shooting she was there! Her partner had called her that night and asked her to meet him by the old railway track and told her to get there urgently, and when she got there she heard shots being fired and shouted out to him but got no answer. She tried calling him on his phone, but again no answer, she waited a while longer but was scared and drove off home after trying to call him again."

"Did she say why she had to meet him?"

"All he told her, Shaun, that something had gone tits up and told her to meet him as soon as possible by the old gate where they walked the dog on the old railway line."

"I don't understand, Kath, why would someone want to kill her for that? As all she did was go there to meet him."

"They checked his phone records and, as he called her last before he died, they think she knows more, and worse than that they actually think she found him and took a bag he was carrying which had a load of diamonds in it!"

Shaun felt the blood drain from his face and immediately rolled up another cig and as he lit it up he said, "Sorry about the language, babe, but fucking hell this is unreal."

He comforted Kath and she asked to use the bathroom, "Yeah, straight up the spiral staircase to your right, babe."

As Kath walked into the house he noticed his hands were shaking and his mouth felt bone dry. He went straight to the kitchen and drank a glass of water, then poured out 2 glasses of coke for him and Kath and took them inside. Kath came down the stairs and he gave her the coke and she sat down on the sofa.

"Bloody hell, I never liked that man of hers," she said, "I knew he was trouble the first time I set eyes on him, there was something about him that made me feel all creepy, but now my girl is in trouble because of that bastard!"

She took a sip of her coke and Shaun asked her again, "Who is going to kill her then?"

"I think it's the people who he stole the diamonds from."

"But you said they knew he called her from his phone just before he died, how would they know that? As only the police would have access to that information as it was them that found him!"

"I honestly don't know, Shaun, but you have a point there."

"Has Beth spoken to the police about this, Kath?"

"I don't know, Shaun, I don't think so, but am all confused."

"Listen, Kath, maybe you need to speak to Beth again as this doesn't seem to add up, maybe she knows more and she is holding back and hiding something, but the police need to know."

Kath looked into Shaun's eyes and said, "All I do know is that they have given her till Friday to hand the diamonds back, otherwise they're going to kill her. Beth has sworn black and blue she has no idea about any diamonds."

"How did they contact her then?"

"They came 'round to the house and ransacked it looking for the diamonds and then threatened her."

"Bloody hell, Kath, it sounds horrendous."

"The day we met in town, Shaun, is the day they came 'round, that's why I had to go home straight away, but she didn't tell me why then, she just said she was really upset."

"But why wait till now, Kath?"

"I don't know Shaun, I just want the whole thing to go away, I cannot stand this any longer."

"Listen Kath, am sure it will be alright, you really need to speak to Beth and she needs to call the police, or at least ask her why she hasn't already spoken to them!"

"I know you have only known me for a few days, Shaun, but could you talk to Beth as you seem to be more switched on to these type of things as I cannot think straight and you seem to ask all the right type of questions!"

"I will try Kath, am used to asking a lot of questions in my job for risk assessments and investigations, but not sure this is a great field for me, but I will give it a go. Am in work tomorrow till 5 so I could come 'round about 6ish, if that's OK? Or is she in yours now?"

"Yes, Shaun, she is staying over."

"Then why don't I come over now, as it appears there isn't much time to lose with this, Kath."

"She may be asleep, Shaun, but yeah let's go back now and I will wake her if she's asleep and ask her to come down and explain," she stood up and gave him a hug, "Thanks Shaun, you're a good man."

He grabbed his car keys, locked up the house and followed Kath back home. Somehow, he was keeping his shit together, but just like when he first found the bag he wanted to know more and more to understand the situation and make sure he was safe; here again he found himself thrown in the middle of a gigantic aftermath of biblical proportions. But once more his mind was now focused on how to resolve the situation and at the same time keep himself out of it. The drive didn't take too long but he had already had a thousand different thoughts running through his mind, his last thought was, *'what if they do kill her!'* He could never look at Kath again as he knew that if he had given the diamonds back like he first thought when he found them, then maybe she wouldn't be in this mess now.

He walked into the house and Kath offered him a drink, "Yeah, tea please, love."

Whilst she was making the tea his mind was focused on staying cool and trying to think of the questions he could ask Beth, "Listen, Kath, I will stay in the garden and have a cig whilst you get Beth."

She went upstairs to get her, and he sat there, thinking some more, and then Beth appeared in front of him.

"Hiya Beth, your mum was telling me that you're in trouble, I just thought I'd come 'round and talk to you and maybe try to understand it and help you if possible? Some of the things your mum told me just didn't add up and was hard to follow.

Kath gave Beth a cup of tea and she sat down next to Shaun, "What do you need to know?" she asked.

"Well, firstly, have you spoken to the police?"

"No, I can't, Shaun."

"Why's that, Beth?"

"His mate, or so called partner, was with the police when they came 'round to tell me he was dead. It was him that told me he was dead and, no sooner had he told me he died, he put his arms around me and whispered in my ear not to mention that he was with him on the few days he went on that trip down south, otherwise we will all be fucked. The other police then took me to one side and asked me all sorts of questions and one of them was if I know what he was doing that night and any idea where he was last week for 3 days, I just said I thought he was at work doing what he does, they left it at that for that night, but by then Craig called 'round."

"Sorry, Beth, but who's Craig?"

"Oh, sorry, that's Paul's partner's name. Well, he called 'round and told me that Paul was doing a big deal that night and it went tits up. He said he wasn't involved in it but did help him with some of the planning and that's why they went to London for 3 days last week and what appeared to be a walk in the park, that night turned into a nightmare. I told Craig that Paul had called me that night and told me to meet him and get there fast as he said he was in the shit, I asked him then why he called me and not him as he helped him plan it! But Craig said he was doing another job that night with the police and that's why he couldn't get to him and as he couldn't get him he must have called me out of desperation. I asked him what was this so called walk in the park all about and he said he was doing a handover with the diamonds as they had a buyer for them and he would have made a huge killing with the deal. I shouted at Craig, saying he should have been there to help him, but again he said he simply couldn't get to him that night. He then mentioned that the investigators will check Paul's phone and see that he called me and told me to stick to the story and say he did call you but only to say that he was working late and he would see me tomorrow, and then said to me again not to mention his name and we will all come out of it OK. I told him I haven't got anything to fear as I've done nothing wrong but he then got angry with me and said "look at your new car and the house he bought you and probably enough money to keep me in all that designer shit I wear for years, you will lose the lot as where do you think all that came from!" I told him to get out the house and leave me alone, he then grabbed me by the neck and said one word from me about him, and my kids won't have a mother and then he asked me if I was sure, I was telling him everything! I told him I hadn't a clue what he was on about and he then asked me if there anything by the gate that I may have picked up! I told him again I didn't have a clue what he was on about and told him to leave the fucking house now and then he threw me to the floor and said again, one word and am dead."

"Bloody hell, Beth, what happened then?"

"Well, the police came 'round the next day and asked me more questions but I stuck to the story as I was told. I was even taken 'round to the police station to give another statement but again I stuck to what I was told. The thing is Shaun, I didn't know what he was doing one day to the next and some weeks I didn't hardly see him at all, and then when he did come home he would often drop a load of money on the table and say "perks of the job!" At first I was petrified as I knew he was a bad cop, but somehow I also found it exciting at the same time and the money kept on coming in and it wasn't just money, it was jewellery with very expensive watches and rings, I've got a safe upstairs with all sorts in it, can you imagine if the police ask me to open that? I think Paul had a safe in his house too, so that's why I cannot tell the police, Shaun."

Shaun looked at Kath and gave her a wink and a reassuring smile and Kath asked, "Does anyone want another brew?"

This was taken up immediately by Shaun and Beth. "Listen, Beth, maybe you need to give me all the stuff in the safe for a while, because they will eventually come 'round and search the place and they will find the safe and ask you to open it and if all that's left in it is, say, just some personal stuff of Paul's then you should be OK, but also tell them that you don't have the combination for the safe as only Paul knew it. That way it would help you distance yourself further from him and his ways! Once the police have an incline that you was benefitting from his actions then am sure they will just dig deeper and deeper, so just stick with the story of not knowing anything other than you thought he was just doing his job as a policeman. The police may try to tie you in on all his other activities but if they have nothing to pin you down to it then, if not anything else, at least they might just charge you with a lesser crime! As for the house and car just say you was serious with each other and you thought it was just normal to be buying a house together."

"The thing is, Shaun, I did know he was up to no good and I don't like to lie, but I have my sons to think of."

"Listen Beth, you have to lie, it's that simple, but for now it's not the police you have to worry about. Tell me more about the day your house was ransacked.

You could see the anger on Beth's face as she said, "3 men just burst in the house and, while 2 was looking all over the place, one stood over me and asked me where the bag was. I thought they meant my handbag at first and pointed to my bag but he said no, the bag with all the stuff in, I told him I didn't have a clue what he was talking about and when the other 2 men came down stairs and said they couldn't find anything, the one standing over me said I have till Friday to hand the bag back or am dead."

"What was the 3 men like, Beth?"

"To be truthful, they was only about 18, maybe 20, years old, and they never took anything from the house and they seemed pretty scared themselves, as one of the them kept shouting, "come on, let's go." I told them the police was coming back to interview me and, as they was leaving, the one guy doing all the talking said, "do the right thing lady, you got till next Friday," and that's why am too scared to tell the police as I was there the night he died and I did know he was bad and also I know he was with Craig them 3 days down south."

"Listen, Beth, give me some time to think this through as I have a feeling Craig has a lot more to do with this. But for now just don't do anything till I get back to you tomorrow."

Beth went upstairs and asked Shaun to come with her whilst she opened the safe, she opened the sliding door of the built in wardrobe and then removed a small section of wood at the back of the wardrobe, the wood had magnets attached to it which kept it in place and to the untrained eye you would never have known it was there. She opened the safe and just like she said there was expensive looking jewellery and at least 10 grand in money and a gun in a holster.

Shaun's eyes looked at the three watches, "Bloody hell, Rolex, all three of them."

"That's nothing," said Beth, "he had more but sold some stuff off and that's when he got me the house."

"Does he have a safe in his house too, Beth?"

"Yes, he has, but he says that's only for his gun which he uses sometimes at work."

Beth put all the stuff into a bag except for the gun and gave it to Shaun, "Wipe all your fingerprints off the safe, Beth, and all around it too, including the false section of wall."

She got a damp cloth and wiped around everywhere and closed the safe and put back the false section of wall and wiped all around that too. He went downstairs with the contents of the safe and told Kath what he was doing.

Beth came downstairs after a short while and said, "All clean now."

He looked over and smiled at Beth and said, "Good, just make sure you don't touch the safe again for now. Listen, am going to get off home now and think it through. I will come 'round tomorrow night, and if I think of anything in the mean time, I will give you a call. Just for curiosity, Beth, have you got Craig's number?"

"Why would you want that, Shaun?"

"Oh, just a thought really, it may come in handy."

"Am not sure," she replied, "but Paul kept a backup of his contacts on the computer."

"Well, if you find it, Beth, send it over to me."

As he walked to the door Kath gave him a big hug, and thanked him for his help. He turned around to Kath and Beth and said, "The two of you get some sleep tonight and worry about this in the morning. Listen, Kath, I have a feeling over this and am sure something can be done."

"I hope so, Shaun, as I just want this all to go away so we all can live our lives. I think we have met for a reason, Shaun, I really do."

"I do too Kath," *'a lot more than you will ever know,'* he thought.

He walked to the car and gave a wave goodbye and fired up the engine and headed home via McDonald's for a latte. The night had flew by and it was now nearly one in the morning. He picked up his latte and pulled in to the car park and, as he sipped at his drink and lit up a cig, he ran all sorts of different scenarios in his mind of what to do next but seemed to be getting nowhere fast. He powered back up the car and drove home.

As soon as he got home he took the contents of the safe upstairs and then took Barney out for a quick walk. Last night the stars shone bright and looked kind of magical but tonight the clouds have come back in.

On getting home, he locked up and put the contents of the safe in the loft alongside the bag and fell fast asleep on getting into bed, as the day and night took its toll.

20th April

Monday

The phone burst into life at 7am and he cancelled the alarm with gusto to stop the alarm, which was the theme of the Xbox game 'Metal Gear Solid' - the alarm was the sound of when you have been spotted, which anyone who has played this game would know that this isn't the sound you want to hear first thing in the morning - which is probably the reason why he unconsciously wakes up most morning before the alarm goes off. He lay there, motionless, as he tried to gather his senses, before dragging himself out of bed and straight to the bathroom.

After throwing some water over his face, he went downstairs and made a brew. He was mentally shattered and took his tea and Barney out to the garden. He lit up a cig and sat there and wondered what on earth was going on in his life. Finding the bag was one thing, and finding Kath was another, but finding the two connected was hard to fathom, and now he is 5 days away from seeing someone killed, which is insane. The rain started to pour down and so he and Barney retreated back inside and he finished his cig with his head out the window to blow the smoke out. After his cig he took a shower and the water hit the right spot as it soothed his aching muscles and refreshed his tiredness. As the water poured over his body he knew he was out of his depth with this latest going on and, like Kath, he too wished it would all just somehow go away, though he knew this wasn't going to go away too easily. He thought for a split moment to walk away from everything, but if he did, he would have Beth's murder on his conscience all his life and he wouldn't be able to look at his beautiful Kath again, especially knowing he could have done something to save her, *'but what on earth can I do?'* he thought, "For fuck's sake, think of something," he shouted to himself in the shower.

On getting out of the shower, and when all bathroom duties were complete, he got himself ready and came down the stairs for another brew. He sat there deep in thought whilst sipping at the hot tea until Barney made it perfectly clear he wanted to go on a walk. Putting his Mac on, he took Barney out in the pouring rain, *'well, 2nd shower this morning,'* he thought to himself as he hit the rain.

On getting back home he took off his wet Mac and dried his hair with a towel and then dried Barney with an old towel, to which Barney thought it was great fun to try to rip the towel to shreds and then not let go of the towel and then run around the house like a lunatic, *'what is it with dogs and water,'* he thought. He put out some food for Barney and then made himself a double espresso, with his beloved cheap coffee maker machine, then headed off to work. The traffic was as mad as ever but the espresso was kicking in and by the time he got to work he was alive and kicking.

He tried to be natural with his colleagues but his secretary Katie could tell something was up, "You OK, Shaun? As you got that sad face on today."

He looked up at Katie, shrugged his shoulders and said, "Oh, I'm OK, I've just had a funny weekend that's all and its left me feeling a bit low."

"Well, you can tell me more about it later when you take me for a coffee," she said.

He smiled at Katie and said, "Yeah, OK kid. How was your weekend, Katie?"

"Same old, same old," she said, "bored out of my head mostly, am definitely getting boring me."

He was finding it hard to concentrate on his work but, just like during the years of trouble with his ex-wife, he managed to put it behind him and get his work done and even join in some office banter.

Looking over at Katie, he gestured with his head to escape the office and she nodded. They headed off to the local cafe and got a butty and a coffee.

"So, what's up, Shaun? As you looked worried sick when I first seen you this morning."

"All I can say, Katie, is that am up to my neck in some deep shit."

"Is it money trouble, Shaun?"

"No, it's not that Katie."

"Wish I could say the same thing," she replied, "as am skint as hell, but then again I always am," she laughed, "so tell me then what's up!"

Shaun let off a huge sigh, "I've, err, met another woman, Katie."

"Oh my God," she said, "well, if you feel like this now, then get rid of her as you don't need another madwoman on your hands."

"No Katie, it's not her, in fact she is wonderful, it's her daughter!"

"Shaun, do not allow her daughter to wreck your relationship just like the last one did."

"She isn't actually, she is just, err, err, oh, fuck it, I will tell you. Did you hear about the shootings in Liverpool a few weeks ago?"

"Yeah, it was bad that, Shaun."

"Well, her daughter is, or should I say was, the dead policeman's girlfriend."

"So I take it it's all heavy times this week with everyone, Shaun?"

"Yes, very much so, Katie," he then told her the whole story of how they met etc., but left out some details such as her daughter's death threats and being mixed up in it all.

"Kath sounds lovely, am so delighted for you, but don't get down over her daughter as she will bounce back eventually, and am sure Kath will be OK too."

Shaun felt Katie wasn't buying the whole thing he just said and made up a reason for being gloomy today by saying there was a big argument yesterday and all hell let loose and he said a few things he regrets now.

She replied by saying, "Well, as long as that's all there is, Shaun, am sure it will be OK. Anyways," she asked, "where is your new suit you bought last week?!"

"Oh, am saving it for when the summer comes along, or at least when it gets a bit warmer. Have a fresh look for the summer I thought."

"Yeah, good idea Shaun. Listen, we better get back to work."

They headed back to work and Katie stopped at nearly every shop in sight to look at new dresses and shoes, *'what is it with women and shoes?'* he thought.

The rest of his day flew by as the office was hectic and people were working in full flow to get done. He grabbed his coat and set off to the car park via the Costa Coffee nearby. He sat in his car with his fresh latte and tried to adjust back to the task in hand with Beth, he slowly sipped his latte, lit up a cig, and let the caffeine and nicotine do its stuff as he sat back in his car seat and tried to think of a solution. He thought about the possibility of just coming out with the whole story to them both and hand over the diamonds to Beth to give back, *'hmm, that could just be the answer,'* he thought.

He fired up the car and started to drive home, and as he did his mind started to think about Craig and what he said to Beth. The more he thought about Craig's actions, the more he felt that he may be setting Beth up, or at least trying to get back what they stole and drop Beth in the shit for it, or maybe he had something to do with Paul's death and, besides having to explain all his whereabouts of late to the police, maybe he is trying to hide the fact he may have been there himself and is linked to the death? As if that was the case, he would be going down for a very long time! *'Geez, I wonder if that's the case,'* he thought, *'as if it is then Beth could be in real trouble here as she already knows too much'.*

He got out the car and opened the front door to be greeted by Barney with his usual sway dance and a toy in his mouth and, as usual, it was lead straight on and out for a walk.

He must have bumped into every dog walker in the estate tonight and on a few occasions had to stop Barney from humping a couple of Shih Tzu dogs,

"I don't know what it is about that breed but Barney just wants to hump them," he apologised to the owner and said, "maybe your dog is in season."

To which the owner replied, "No, not in season, I just think your dog is a randy old git," which made them both laugh.

He got to the playing field and, as no other dogs were in sight, he let Barney off the lead to roam around the field. As he watched Barney run around, he sat himself on a small wall, lit up a cig and thought about how much his life has changed in the last 10 crazy days. He had hardly thought about the ex-wife, and as for all the loneliness and sadness of being alone for the first time in his life, that seemed a long, long, time ago. He still had the anger in him when he thought about his ex-wife's evil daughter but knew in time she would get her rewards for being a total bitch, and maybe in some ways she had done him a favour by getting him away from all that. He managed a little laugh as he thought of the way he lived with all of them and how he has a chance to live his life to the full once more and be himself now and felt blessed in meeting Kath. He looked around the field to check on Barney and then his mind drifted back to finding the bag, the money, and the diamonds, and how by finding the bag it has brought him to Kath. He would gladly give the lot up just to be with Kath. He shouted Barney back over to him, clipped the lead on him and started to walk home. He started to think more about the coincidence of finding the bag and then Kath and Beth and started to let his mind wonder about maybe if there was some sort of spiritual thing going on here and wondered if another force was guiding him to help them. He had a strong belief in life after death, or at least that the spirit still lives, and maybe this was Paul's spirit trying to do one last decent thing to save Beth and he had chosen him to find the bag! A cold shiver ran down his body just at the thought of it, but somehow he likened to the thought of it too, as if he was being guided by another force, then maybe he and everyone else would come out OK.

On getting home he fed Barney and made a few ham butties for himself and sat there and thought more about finding a way of making it right. He then got a text from Kath saying: *"You still coming over tonight?."* He quickly replied: *"Yes, but only if there is plenty of biscuits available and a cuppa!"* Her reply was instant too: *"Biscuits tea and my lips waiting x."* Shaun closed his eyes for a split second as he thought of her soft lips and let out a little moan. He quickly got back to thinking of the threat on Beth and he was convinced more so than ever that Craig had a lot to do with everything and somehow the answer lay with him.

He demolished his butties, grabbed a quick shower and had time for another brew and a cig outside in the garden. He started to think of the 3 day undercover journey Paul and Craig went on and Paul being left alone for the last leg of the plot for the, so called, walk in the park to collect and drop off the merchandise, *'if they was together in this, then they would have been together that night am pretty much sure about that as they was partners in work, and also in crime, maybe now the people who was doing the hand over are threatening him and he is telling them that Beth has the diamonds to try and save his own arse or he is simply trying to get them back for himself!'*

He set off in the car to Kath's, and as he pulled up outside her house she came outside to greet him. She looked every inch a P.A in a law firm with her business clothes on.

"Hey, you look great Kath, love the clothes."

"Oh, I haven't got changed yet, I've had too much to do but am glad you like them."

"Oh, I do," he replied quickly, "you look so authoritative in them, I may need you to wear them for me one night and take some notes for me!"

She laughed and said, "Get your mind out the gutter, Shaun, as Beth is here," she gently kissed him and they headed inside the house.

Beth came into view and smiled, "I got Craig's number and his address."

"Hey, that's good Beth, let me have it." He put the info in his phone and then walked into the living room where Kath, as promised, had the biscuits waiting for him.

"I will bring in the tea now, Shaun."

"Thanks, lovely," he replied.

Beth sat down next to him and said she had slept well last night and it was a relief telling them both what had been going on.

"I bet it was Beth. Listen kid, I think Craig is up to his neck in all of this, and I also think he may have been involved in the gang and is setting you up. It's possible that the men that came round to rough you up may have been sent by Craig to test you and also see if you did have the diamonds and, I may be wrong, but I think he may have been there on the night Paul died and is trying to cover his tracks! You know all about him and his involvement with it all and it puts you at danger with him."

Beth quickly stated, "He did warn me at the funeral and told me to keep my mouth shut."

"Yeah, he sounds a lovely man, Beth. Where are the kids, by the way?"

"Oh, they're upstairs watching the tele for an hour before the go to sleep."

"Geez, they're quiet for 2 young kids."

"Yeah, they're really good most nights," she replied.

Kath came in with the tea and she said, "I think you're right about Craig. He has a lot to do with everything, in fact, I think he is behind the bloody lot of it!"

"Do you think he may have really been there that night Paul died?" asked Beth.

"Yeah, I do, Beth. Something isn't right with his story and the threats with you plus the way he was with you by getting angry… I think he is up to no good, this man."

"We could test the water with him, Beth, by you calling him on the phone and saying you need to speak to him and ask him to call around at 10 tonight. And if he asks why, just say you're not saying anything over the phone but to just get 'round here as Paul did say something else on the phone that night!"

"But what about the kids, Shaun?"

"Just leave them here with Kath tonight, and I will come with you and listen from upstairs, and if it starts to get out of hand, I will call you on the phone. So make sure you tell him that your mum's boyfriend is going to pick you up and will call you first to let you know he is on his way, as hopefully he won't want to hang around much longer then as he wouldn't want anyone knowing he was there!"

"But what do I say when he comes 'round?"

"Tell him about the threat this Friday, and the gang that came 'round the house, and ask him how the gang knew about the phone call from Paul as only him and the police would have known that, so he must have been behind it! And mention that Paul did say something else on the phone just before he put the phone down he said, "it was Craig, it's Craig.""

"What good will that do?" asked Beth.

"Well, if he has anything to do with it, he will shit himself, as if you mention that to the police, he will be arrested and re-interviewed and I doubt he will be serving God, queen and country much longer, but more like staying at Her Majesty's Pleasure for a very long time!"

"But what about the gang that's coming on Friday for me, Shaun?"

"I think he is behind that too, and if you tell him that, then maybe he can change all that. But I think there is no gang and he just got some lads 'round to scare you to see if you did have the diamonds and, as you haven't, then he is looking at making sure his name isn't brought up in it all as maybe he had a part in Paul's death too."

"But, Shaun, what happens if he hasn't a connection with the gang and he isn't behind it all?"

"Well, Beth, I will need to use plan B."

"And what's plan B, Shaun?"

"I haven't thought of that yet, am afraid, but I feel I am right so just call him now as the police and the gang, if they do exist, may be interested in the game this bastard is playing!"

Beth called the number from her mobile and hit loud speaker, he instantly said, "What do you want?"

"I need to see you tonight at 10 at my house," said Beth, "as I need to tell you something that Paul said on the phone that night."

There was a slight pause and he replied by saying, "OK, cya at 10," and he hung up.

"Well, that's got his attention," said Kath, "he also had her number in his phone too as he knew it was her straight away!"

"That's true," Beth said, "he has never called me before, maybe he had it from Paul."

Shaun replied by saying, "Maybe he made it his business to know your number, Beth, and these undercover cops have it all down so maybe he could even be tracking you on the phone or monitoring your calls!"

"Geez, that's a scary thought," said Beth as she looked at Shaun and said, "am scared."

"I'm scared too, Beth, but if this goes right, then maybe he will back off and all will be OK. When I was young lad I got into all sorts of trouble and always found a way out of it, but that was a long time ago. The last 10 years or so all I've done is carry out risk assessments and safety reports."

"You should have been a policeman," said Kath, "as your mind thinks well."

"I don't know about that Kath, but I do know that the root cause of this points to Craig every time."

Kath put her arm around Beth and said, "Will you be OK, baby? As if that bastard does anything to you, then I will kill him myself, Oh my God, Shaun, you sure this will be OK as he may try to kill her and you too!"

"Don't worry, babe, he won't do that," he thought to himself *'well I hope not!'*

"Am going to get the kids asleep now," said Beth and went upstairs to see them.

He went outside for a cig with Kath and he reassured her things would be OK. After a while Beth came down the stairs and said the kids were now fast asleep.

"Well, I think it's time we headed off to yours now, Beth."

"Please look after yourselves," said Kath.

"Don't worry, lovely, you promised me tea, biscuits, and your lips. Well, I've only had the tea and the biscuits, so am coming back for them lips."

Beth looked at Shaun with an expression of 'what the hell are you like' and shook her head, it worked for Kath though as she blew him a kiss.

Beth climbed into Shaun's car and said, "Geez, how the hell do you get in and out of this thing all of the time?"

"Yeah, the Celica is low, but once you're in your laughing."

"Your car needs a bloody good cleaning, Shaun, it's filthy. I guess you wouldn't mind me lighting up a cig as I couldn't make any more mess than what it is!"

"Of course you can smoke as long as you don't use the ashtray as that ashtray is as good as new and hasn't been used once."

"I can tell," she said, "by the state of the floor," and they both laughed as they both lit up a cig and dropped down the windows to let the smoke and ash out.

"Why are we going this way, Shaun, as I live the other side."

"Oh, I need to go to mine first to get something, and then we will fly 'round to yours."

Shaun ran up the stairs of his house and quickly opened the loft, took out the gun and placed in down the back of his jeans, and gave Barney a little stroke, and then locked back up and got back into the car.

Shaun then said to Beth, "Right then, you can be my human sat nav, take me to yours."

Beth seemed pretty calm for what she was about to do, *'but I guess with her having a fella like she did she had become pretty streetwise and could look after herself a bit'.*

"I live just down this road here," she pointed about halfway down.

Shaun looked around and thought to himself how nice the neighbourhood was, "Nice here, kid."

"Yeah, I like it," she said.

"Listen, Beth, I will stop the car well before yours so he doesn't see any cars outside yours as we don't want to make him feel suspicious or clocking my car."

He pulled up the car and they walked the rest of the way which was about 100 yards from her house. She reached for her keys and opened the door and turned some lights on. It was a very modern house, but a house that you could see kids lived in as there were toys just about everywhere, including a little 3-wheeler bike in the hall. It was now 9pm and Shaun asked for a brew and they then went over what she needed to say a few times.

"I am going to go up the stairs now and sit on the landing just in case he comes early. You will be fine, Beth, just remember to let him know right at the start that I will be ringing you to say am on my way to pick you up."

Shaun went upstairs and placed a chair on the landing and sat down and waited, his brain was thinking at the speed of light as the minutes ticked past.

After about 30 minutes Beth walked up the stairs, "What's up, Beth? You OK?"

"Yeah, I just need to pee!"

"Oh, OK then."

The tension was definitely building, as when Beth flushed the toilet he felt his muscles clench in fright, *'fucking hell,'* he thought, *'what the hell am I doing, but it's too late to run off now'*.

Beth crept past him, and Shaun asked, "Why are you creeping, Beth?"

"I don't know," she said, "I just didn't want to make any noise."

He smiled at her and said, "Stupid girl," and a smile came to their faces, "look, Beth, try to be yourself."

"I will, don't worry, Shaun."

10 o'clock came and passed and Shaun's heart rate was now going up by each minute and wiped the sweat of his brow, he felt physically sick at the thought of what could happen and stared at the gun in his hands, fully knowing that this could go all wrong and, not only Beth, but his life could be over too in an instant. A voice in his head was telling him to calm down which kind of spooked him a bit as he felt the voice in his mind wasn't his, but within seconds he gained control of himself and became calm again. Looking at his watch it was now 10:15 when there was a knock on the door!

Craig walked straight in and said, "What's up?"

She told him of the threat she had and how she has till Friday or else.

"What's that got to do with me?" he asked.

Craig seemed agitated and looked menacing as he stared at Beth, Beth replied by saying, "Well, only you and the police knew I was there that night, so why would a gang come 'round to the house and threaten me? Unless you had something to do with it?!"

Craig angrily replied by saying, "Listen here, bitch, you just do as I fucking tell you and, like I said, I don't have a fucking clue why they came here."

Shaun listened carefully as she told him to keep his hands off her. "My mum's fella is going to ring me and pick me up soon," she said, "so you better not rough me up."

Craig's voice was now sounding even more angry as he said, "What's all this about Paul saying something else?"

"Listen, Craig, you better sort all this out or am going to the police, as just before the phone went dead that night Paul mentioned your name!"

"What did he say? He just told me to hurry up and pick him up and then said, "it's Craig"!"

"What about me?!" Craig shouted angrily.

"I don't know," she said, "he just said it's Craig."

"First of all, bitch, you mention this to the police and I will fuck you up good style myself."

"Well, I will tell the gang then," shouted Beth.

Craig laughed and said, "You think for 1 minute you're going to blow me up to the police or them cockney fuckers, then am going to take great pleasure in hurting you and the kids. Got it?"

With that Shaun rang Beth's number. "Who the fuck is that?" said Craig.

"It's my mum's fella, like I said, he would call before he comes 'round to pick me up. He will be here in 5 minutes."

"You better not go to the police with this," he said again, "as I will carry out what I've threatened."

Beth then shouted at him saying, "Well, you better sort all this gang shit out as I am not going down for something I haven't done, and if I go down, you do too, got it? And while you're there Craig, tell me where the fucking diamonds are!"

You could hear the slap across her face all over the house.

She shouted, "stop it" and Shaun instantly stood up and held the gun firm in his hand.

He waited for a further few seconds in case he kept on attacking her, but it appeared that the slap was all she was getting for now. But Shaun's mind was so clearly focused on the job in hand and there was no way he was going to let her get hurt anymore. He put the gun in his left hand as he reached for the phone with his right hand and called her once more, his hands were trembling and for a split second he nearly dropped the phone which would have given himself away upstairs, but somehow managed to keep hold of it.

"My mum's fella is here so fuck off Craig or am going to tell everyone about you."

"Open the back door to let me out, you bitch, and one word and your kids are going to get it too."

Beth opened the back door, and as he ran out she quickly locked the door again and went to the hallway. Shaun put the gun back inside his jacket and ran down the stairs and quickly opened and slammed shut the front door to make sure people heard the door being closed, just in case he was hiding and listening out for it around the corner.

"Bloody hell, Beth, way to go. You really did well, get something cold on that face of yours as it looks pretty sore where he slapped you."

"It is sore, but fuck him," she said, "his face was livid when I mentioned his name from Paul, it looked like he had seen a ghost when I said Paul had said it's Craig! I know it's him behind it all Shaun I can just tell it's all him."

"OK Beth, listen, just lock up the place and tell me all about it in the car as we better get back to your mum as she will be worried sick."

As they walked down the street Beth's eyes was looking everywhere in case he was still around.

He opened the door of the car for Beth to get in and said to her, "You can light up another cig as you bloody deserve it."

He got in the car and fired up the engine. He noticed Beth's hands shaking as she tried to light up the cigarette, "I cannot help you light that up as my hands are shaking too!" he said.

They both had a little laugh and then drove off. As she took her first pull of the cig you could see that she was calming down instantly and she said, "Bloody hell, Shaun, that was insane. I was shitting myself at first but when I mentioned Paul I just boiled up inside, I meant everything I said, if I go down, so will that bastard, but what now Shaun?"

He steered hard onto the road and said, "Well, he did say he was going to call you tomorrow night, so I guess the next move is his, but I can guarantee you that he will be doing some serious thinking now."

They pulled up outside Kath's house and Kath came running out, "Is everything OK?" she shouted.

He nodded his head and said, "Take Beth inside, she needs a strong cup of tea."

As Kath and Beth walked into the house he took the gun out of his jacket and placed it under the seat of the car then quickly followed them inside.

Kath noticed the red mark on Beth's face courtesy of the slap she received from Craig, "Oh my," she said, "that must hurt."

"Yes, it does, Mum, but I think he may be hurting more himself right now as I told him straight what I will do if anything comes from this."

Kath put a cold flannel on Beth's face to ease the swelling as it was starting to come up just below the eye. Kath looked over to Shaun and said, "So, do you think Beth won't be hurt now and he will tell them gangsters to back off?"

"Hopefully, Kath, but let's see what happens tomorrow when he calls."

Beth walked over to Shaun and said she was still shaking a bit from the ordeal and he replied by saying he was too as whilst he was upstairs listening to it all he was totally crapping himself, "So God knows how you felt like Beth, you done well kid."

"Anyways, am off to bed now," she said and gave him a hug and said, "thanks."

She gave her mum a hug too and off she went upstairs and, as she did, she looked over to Kath and said, "Oh, you may be able to give him them lips you owe him now," and laughed as she went up the stairs, they all had a little laugh which helped ease the tension.

"You want a coffee Shaun?"

"Yeah, go on, Kath," he said.

He followed her to the kitchen and, as she reached up to get 2 cups for the coffee, he placed his arms around her and kissed the back of her neck, "Mmm, that's nice baby," she said and turned to face him.

They kissed some more and she reached over and turned off the kitchen light. The intensity hit new heights as they made love against the kitchen worktop.

"Oh my, Shaun, that was fantastic."

"Yes it was, Kath, in fact, that was something else. I think the whole experience and excitement of the night caught up with me and I felt like screaming at the end," laughed Shaun.

Eventually the coffee was made and they went to sit out in the garden, lit up a cig each and spoke some more about the night. Then he reminded Kath how late it was now and how he had better get off home so they both can have some sleep.

As he drove home his eyes were looking all around, in case he was being followed, but there were no cars on the road this evening and as he got closer to home his heart started pounding in his chest as he noticed a police car coming alongside him at the lights, 'oh shit,' he thought. He brought his car to a stop at the lights and looked over, but the 2 policeman in the car didn't even bother looking at him as they were totally engrossed in conversation with each other and as soon as the lights started to change the police car sped off as if they had somewhere to go in a hurry. He let out a big sigh of relief and continued to drive home, and as he reached his driveway he took out the gun from under the seat, put it back in his jacket and went inside.

He put the gun back into the loft and took Barney out for a very quick walk around the estate. His mind was still trying to take in all the goings on of the night and thinking about Craig and wondering where to go next with it all.

On getting back home he could feel a tiredness from hell descending upon him so he quickly locked up and jumped straight into bed and was asleep before his head hit the pillow.

21st April

The phone alarm went into overdrive as he slowly came around from being in a deep sleep, the last few days has been taking its toll on him. As he slowly reached over to switch the annoying sound off the phone, he sat up against the side of the bed and double checked the time it was 07:00. *'Gone are the days of waking up before the alarm,'* he thought as he trudged into the bathroom. He ached in places that he didn't know existed and his thoughts went back to making love to Kath against the worktop as a smile came to his face, "Am going to have to get in shape for this woman," he laughed and got straight into the shower and let the warm water do its magic and soothe his tired body.

His thoughts then went back to being upstairs on the landing with the gun whilst Beth was downstairs having it out with Craig and he let out a small laugh and shook his head, *'what the bloody hell am doing? In fact, who the bloody hell do I think I am? Am running round like Clint Eastwood!'* As the water ran over his body he kind of likened to the idea of what he had become and the excitement was like something he had never experienced before, and even though his body ached with fatigue his mind had never felt so alive, this was so different from the life he has had, where the biggest threat he had in the last 12 months was greenflies attacking his plants in the garden.

With all bathroom duties complete, he went downstairs and made the first brew of the day and made a big fuss of

Barney, "Look what you got me into, Barnes," he said, "it's all your fault your dad is running round with a gun in his jacket."

He sat in the garden with his brew, rolled up the cig and let the caffeine and nicotine do their work. Looking at his phone he noticed a message from Kath saying: *"How's my lovely man this morning and thanks again for helping Beth, you coming up tonight at 7 xx."* He tapped in the reply: *"Am good thanks babe and if Craig calls Beth, you need her to contact me as soon as possible, cya at 7 my lovely lady xx."* As he hit the send button he took the last swig of his tea, headed inside, and took Barney out for a walk.

It felt a lot warmer today as he strolled around the estate and all the aches, pains and tiredness had gone.

On getting home he fed Barney, got changed and went off to work. He left for work a little earlier today as he wanted to leave work that bit earlier. He stopped by the Tesco garage to grab a vendor Costa latte and a croissant. The hardest part of his day was about to begin, as how do you eat a freshly cooked croissant whilst driving without making a total mess in your car with the crumbs? He had tried all sorts of different ways of eating them without success, even putting the plastic bag towards his chin doesn't stop the flakes of croissant breaking off on his suit and the seat of the car. He looked across at a car next to him at the lights and a woman driver smiled at him, *'she obviously had a croissant or 2 in her car herself and appreciated my efforts to catch the flakes'.*

On arrival at his work, he parked the car and set about the day as normal. The other staff in the office weren't buying it though, they could all see that somehow something was not right.

When he offered to make the tea for everyone, one of his colleagues asked, "What's up Shaun? You're not yourself, mate."

"I'm OK thanks, just some heavy shit going on at home, but don't worry, I'm OK mate."

He knew that all the office would probably be asking him the same thing all day, as it was clear he wasn't himself, so when he made the tea for everyone he said, "Listen up, guys," all the heads in the office looked up towards him, "to save telling all of you the same story, I'm OK," he said, "just some weird shit going on at home, but the main thing is am seeing a new woman and she is wearing me out!"

They all laughed and Andy from Wigan jokingly shouted some obscenity at him and the ones who could understand his thick Wigan accent laughed along too, "You know am only kidding," said Andy, "I love you really."

Shaun smiled over, as his friendship with Andy was good, "I know mate, but listen, no worries, all is good."

They bought this excuse and, after a few more minutes of banter, they all quietly got on with their own day. Shaun, however. was checking his phone for texts from Kath or Beth, but none came.

Katie was off work today so he went for lunch on his own and, sitting outside the cafe with his latte and tuna crunch panini, he texted Kath: *"Hey how's your day babe, am just having lunch and thinking of you x."* His reply was soon coming: *"I'm OK thx honey, I just want to go home though as I feel like a ticking time bomb, miss you x. "* He knew how she felt as his nerves have been tested to the limit from the moment he found the bag and the terror of finding the body, though this somehow didn't compare to those emotions but more like a sustained adrenaline rush and, just like a toothache, this wasn't going away. His mind was switched on but he knew that Craig's actions would determine the result and he let his mind wander to the possibility of telling the police now, at least Beth would be safe, *'though probably inside a prison cell for a while and me too for that matter and that is one thing I couldn't do is time inside prison'*.

He headed back to work and got stuck in with his tasks, finished the day earlier and headed for home.

The drive was a nightmare as Edge Lane, which led to the start of the M62, was total gridlock. The only answer was to pull into a service station, buy a Pepsi and a packet of crisps and munch his way through the traffic. He noticed a billboard saying 'Be all you can be' and he laughed as he knew he was being all he could possibly be right now.

On eventually making it home he opened the door and Barney did his usual sway dance and brought him a toy in his mouth.

Clipping on the lead he took him out for a quick walk, but today the walk was cut short as he got a call from Beth, "Shaun, he is coming 'round to see me at 8 tonight."

"Did he say anything else, Beth?"

"No, that's all."

"OK, Beth, are the kids going 'round to your mum's?"

"Yeah, going to do that soon, Shaun, as mum will be home any minute now."

"OK then, Beth, I will come over as soon as I get back home and get changed etc., cya later."

He finished off the walk with Barney, got home and gave Barnes some dinner and then got a quick wash and changed. He went straight out to garden with Barney, lit up a cig and tended to his plants, whilst his mind thought of the meet tonight. He thought about the gun, last night it had just seemed the thing to do, but somehow today it didn't. He hadn't fired a proper gun all his life, though as a lad he had a few airguns and an air rifle, and after checking out YouTube on the Glock 19 he knew he could fire the thing now, but whether he would hit anything with it was another thing.

After his cig he went back inside and checked the internet one more time to look over the Glock 19. As he watched it being demonstrated he knew this wasn't for him as he watched carefully how to fire it and check the chamber, *'this was one hell of a deadly weapon,'* he thought, *'in the right hands'*. But in his hands he would probably shoot himself in the foot, but this wasn't a noisy neighbour or someone who just needs a good pasting but a probable killer who wouldn't think twice about taking out Beth. *'Bloody hell, what have I become?'* he thought as he put the gun back in his jacket.

He locked up and headed for Kath's and as he pulled up on the driveway Kath came outside to greet him,

"Hiya, lovely," he said.

She gave him a quick kiss and they went inside, "You OK, Beth?"

"Yeah, I'm OK thanks, Shaun. Just wish I knew what he wants tonight."

"Me too, Beth, but, err, we better get going."

"I feel so helpless," said Kath, "I really wish I could somehow help."

"You are helping," said Shaun, "just by being here. Just keep your phone on and I will let you know how it went as soon as he has gone."

They headed to the car, waved to Kath and drove off, "Does your phone have a record facility on it, Beth?"

"Am not sure, Shaun."

"Well, have a look for it then, as it may be an idea to record what he is saying."

"What good will that do, Shaun?"

"You never know, Beth, it may just come in handy for the police, if necessary."

She got to work looking for it on her phone and said, "Hey, I've found it!"

"Great, Beth, so suss it out and learn how to use it."

They both lit up a cig and, for a few moments, there was silence in the car as they drove to hers. He pulled up the car in the same spot and they headed to the house.

Stepping inside he then said to Beth, "Listen, if he wants you to go anywhere with him, say no, as the kids cannot be left by themselves, and if he asks where your car is, just tell him your mum is bringing it 'round later."

Just then Beth's phone rang and as she picked it up she gestured to Shaun that it was him. She listened to what Craig had to say and said "Oh, OK, but what can I tell them that you can't tell them? I don't like this, Craig," she listened to what he said next and then put the phone down.

"They want to meet me on Thursday night."

"Who does, Beth?"

"The gang," she replied, "Craig said he has sorted something out but they still want to meet me."

"Where you supposed to meet them, Beth?"

"He said to meet them all in the car park in Stanley Park at 10:30."

"I'm not sure I like this, Beth, as how did he sort it? Did he conjure some diamonds out of thin air?"

"Well, he may have them, Shaun."

'If only you knew, Beth,' he thought, "Well, maybe he has, but it doesn't seem right as you have no value to them if you haven't got the diamonds and they wouldn't risk being seen by you too, no, am not having this, Beth. Did Craig say anything else?"

"No, he just said he sorted it, and just stick to the same story if the police ask me any further questions."

"Sorry Beth, am not buying this, to meet in a park at night doesn't make sense."

"Why, Shaun?"

"Well, they know where you live, they have already been to your house when the 3 of them came 'round, so why not come 'round again? So, am sorry, something is going down here. Look, Beth, am no detective or a bloody criminal, but if I wanted to meet someone who I already knew, I would simply walk through the front door! They also know you haven't been to the police so it doesn't add up! Come on, let's go back to your mum's."

Beth locked up and they headed to the car, the two of them were locked in silence as they got inside the car. They both lit up a cig and Beth asked Shaun what he was thinking, "Am thinking this isn't good, Beth. This gang just want their diamonds back, yet with a call from Craig it's all sorted?"

"They may simply believe I haven't got them, Shaun, and Craig has convinced them too."

"Well, maybe, Beth, but everything inside me is telling me this isn't right."

As they got to Kath's Beth got out and he quickly placed the gun under the seat of the car and stepped out. They explained to Kath what had happened and she felt it wasn't right too.

He stepped into the garden and his mind was in overdrive trying to think it through, "You OK, Shaun?" asked Kath.

"Yeah, I'm OK, babe, am just trying to work it out, but I don't like it, Kath, it all feels wrong."

"Would you like a coffee, Shaun?"

"If you don't mind, Kath, am going to head off home and think this through as I don't want to scare you more than you already are, but it feels even more dangerous this now. Listen, you look after Beth tonight and let me think it through and I will call you tomorrow and let you know what I think the best thing to do is."

"Oh, OK Shaun, will you call me later before you go to bed?"

"Yeah I will, Kath."

He said his goodbyes and told Beth not to worry but if she gets any further calls or messages, she must contact him straight away. He gave Kath a little kiss on the cheek and left the house, his mind deep in thought and he felt very anxious about it all.

On getting home, he put away the gun and sat in the garden with a brew and thought it through some more, before taking Barney for a quick walk.

Barney was really happy to see him, as maybe he wasn't giving him his full attention of late, and he pulled hard on the lead as they walked. As they walked he thought of the last few days and ran over the meeting in the park in his mind. As he got to the playing field he let Barney of the lead and sat on the wall, his mind was numb. A woman was shouting at her small child who must have wandered off too far and he came scurrying back towards her. She didn't have a Liverpool accent, in fact it sounded foreign, the boy then held his mother's hand as they walked away. It was this moment that made him think about what Craig said to Beth when he said he didn't care about them Cockney fuckers.

He quickly called Kath and said, "Hey, love, is Beth still there as I need to speak to her?"

"Yeah, she is still here, I will ask her to come to the phone for you."

"Hiya, Shaun, what's up?"

"Listen Beth, I was thinking about the day that gang came 'round to your house, did they have southern accents?"

"I don't think so, Shaun."

"Think hard Beth, did they?"

"Err, well, the one that was standing by me he had a Liverpool accent am sure of it as when he was calling the other 2 lads back his voice was, err, well it was deffo a Liverpool accent, Shaun."

"Did they actually take anything at all, Beth?"

"No, they just tipped out a few drawers and left, why you asking, Shaun?"

"It's OK Beth, am just curious and had a thought. Look, I will let you know more later, tell your mum I will give her a call later."

"OK, Shaun. Laters."

Shaun was now thinking about the gang from London, *'why would they use 3 scallys from Liverpool to look for the diamonds?'* He thought of this over and over again until he came to the conclusion that they wouldn't. They would come up themselves, and Beth wouldn't be here now if they thought she had them as they would have beaten her to within an inch of her life to get them back. This was more like a scare tactic, which wouldn't be used by any serious gang for something like this, but maybe Craig is behind this too! *'Maybe he was using these 3 guys to scare her so not to go to say anything to the police and at the same time trying his hand in case she did have the diamonds! He knows now she hasn't got them, but he also knows she knows he was definitely involved in all of this, so why meet up on Thursday?'* Barney in the meantime was barking like a lunatic, he quickly snapped himself out of the trance he was in, "Hey, Barney, come back here, mate."

It seemed like Barney had met his match in an old tomcat who wasn't backing off at all and Barney was stuck to the spot barking at him, "Come on mate," he said and as he clipped the lead back on his collar and pulled him away, "you met your match there, mate, you little coward. Come on, let's get you home."

As soon as he got back home he called Kath, "Hey babe, I've had a thought, can I come back over to see you and Beth?"

"Yeah, sure, Shaun. Have you eaten anything yet?"

"To be truthful, Kath, I haven't hardly ate much all day."

"Well, let me make something up for you then."

"Thanks Kath, I will explain it all to you when I get there, cya soon, babe."

Locking up the house, he drove quickly around to Kath's and, again, she was on the step waiting for him. He gave her a quick hug and went inside.

"I've made you some sandwiches and a brew, Shaun."

"Mmm cheers, babe, am starving, thanks for that."

He told Kath and Beth what he thought and told them that he felt Thursday night wasn't going to be too good for Beth and explained the reasons why.

"But what now, Shaun?"

"Well, he obviously doesn't want you to talk to anyone as he is up to his neck in it, and probably not just with the police but maybe the underworld too, and one word from you would mean curtains for him one way or another. As if he gets locked up by the police, then the criminals have their own ways to get to him in there, so either way he is going to get fucked, plus no one likes a cop in prison too so he won't last 5 minutes in there."

"So, what are you trying to say, Shaun?" asked Kath, "Do you think he may try to kill Beth?"

Shaun looked at Kath and said, "I think you are both in danger, as if he did kill Beth, he would more than likely come for you too, the same night, as he cannot afford to take the chance you would say something too."

Kath replied by saying, "But if he has Beth's word she wasn't going to say nothing, then surely he will leave her alone?"

"Listen, Kath, people like him don't look at things that way."

"Do you think we should call the police then and tell them the whole lot of it?"

Shaun probably knew it was the right thing to do but somehow he couldn't afford to be a part of it, as if his secret came out then, yes, he may save Beth but would probably lose Kath as a result, "I will have another think about it, Kath, and let you know tomorrow."

He walked into the garden, rolled up a cig and thought, *'shit, what do I do now?'* He knew he had to do the right thing as he was way out of his depth now with all of this. The way he felt for Kath and seeing what a lovely person she was, he simply couldn't allow anything to happen to her or Beth. He did everything to keep the bag a secret but the one thing he didn't count on was love.

"More tea, Shaun?"

"Yeah, go on, Kath."

She brought the tea out and put it on the table outside and said, "A penny for your thoughts?"

He looked at Kath and smiled and said, "My thoughts are getting clearer now and I think I know what to do, can you ask Beth to come outside?"

Beth came out and he told them both to sit down, "Listen, the only way to stop this getting out of hand now is to inform the police," they all lit up a cig as if someone had just put a sign up saying 'light up now', "I think he is going to harm Beth and possibly you Kath as he cannot afford anything to come out and the best way to do that is to silence you both. So, the best thing to do is speak to the police, but not just anyone in the police but maybe Paul's and Craig's boss as he may listen to what we have to say and he would be more than interested in what was going on in his unit! Plus he may be a bit more helpful. The one thing you cannot say to them, Beth, is about the days Paul would throw money at you and all the jewellery stuff, simply leave all that out but stick to the story of how you didn't know what he was doing half of the time, but you know he and Craig went to London for 3 days and then tell them all about the threats and Craig's admission at the meetings. I will keep the money you had in the safe and the jewellery for you, so if a rainy day does come along in the future then happy days!"

"Are you going to tell the police, Shaun, or shall we?"

"Well, I was hoping to stay out of it for obvious reasons, but I guess that's not going to happen now, so yes I will speak to them. Can you look for Paul's boss's number Beth?"

"Yeah, I will look now, Shaun."

"It's OK, Beth, have a look later and call me when you have it as I still want to think of a few things first before I call him.

"Do you think I will go to prison for all of this, Shaun?" asked Beth.

"Phew, that I am not sure, but you have held back information, in fact very important information so they could charge you with a shedload of stuff. And as for the house etc. being bought by funny money, well, I just don't know. Though you stick to your side of the story and say you was simply buying the house together for the future and you didn't think anything was wrong, then maybe you have a chance of keeping the house."

"Fuck the house, Shaun. I would rather lose that than go to jail!"

"Listen, am going to get off home again and think it over. Don't forget to get me that name and number of his boss and let me know later and I will call you tomorrow about 12 o'clock, OK?"

"Am glad we are telling the police," said Kath, "as I feel so much safer now."

"Well, Kath, let's just hope his boss isn't like Craig or Paul!"

"Oh Shaun, why did you say that, I will be more worried now!"

"Am sorry, Kath, don't worry he won't be like them," 'well I hope not,' he thought.

He gave Kath a kiss and said goodbye to Beth and drove home deep in thought.

On getting home he made a brew and sat on the sofa. He knew he could do no more, and the last 2 days of running around Liverpool with a Glock 19 handgun was nothing far short of madness and he was living his life on the edge. The cash, the diamonds, and a beautiful woman has now turned into a web of crime and he is right in the middle of it all and in one wrong turn tomorrow he could lose the lot. The option of letting the meet happen on Thursday was simply not there now and, for once, he felt his body resign to the fact that life as he knew it may be coming to an end. He noticed Barney staring at him and, patting him on the head, he said, "What's up mate, do you know something I don't, Barney?"

Shaun took out a pen and some paper and wrote down how he found the bag and why he didn't go to the police with it and how he met Kath and how much he felt for her and all he was doing was trying to help, he wrote it all down in case his own crime was revealed and hoped one day Kath and his family may understand. As he was writing the letter a tear dropped onto the paper and he held his head in his hands. He tried to pull himself together, it wasn't just losing the money or the shame it would bring on his own daughters and son, but it was losing the dream he had where he and his family could live well and the dream of happiness that he had longed for so much over the years which seemed only a dream months ago to suddenly become a reality in the last few weeks could be gone quicker than it came. He finished the letter and then gave Kath a call and told her he was knackered and going to have an early night but would call her in the morning,

"Shaun, you have been a pillar of strength for us both, I cannot thank you enough and I don't want you to think am getting all heavy on you, especially with all this stuff going on, but I honestly think the world of you and in such a short space of time I feel I have known you all my life."

"Thanks, Kath, I feel the same too. I could look in to your eyes forever, babe. You sleep well, my lovely lady, and I will call you in the morning."

He put the phone down and went off to bed. As he lay there he took a trip down memory lane in his mind and thought about his father who would be shaking his head up there right now and his lovely mother, for whom he could never do any wrong. What he wouldn't do right now to have a cup of tea and a cig with his mum who loved her cigs and cups of tea and she would tell him the stories of when she was a young girl in wartime England and they would laugh and be sad together, but no matter how bad a situation was, somehow his mum always found a smile and a positive view on things. Even lying in bed now he had a smile on his face. His mind then drifted into the wilderness of his failed 2nd marriage, but rather than think of the painful experience of it, he concentrated on one moment, a special moment with her, and he wished her well in his mind. But then he drifted into thoughts of the last year or so on his own of just waking up and going to work and then home to go to bed over and over again without anything else in-between, it was like he was a zombie for so long, and it didn't sit easy with him but he couldn't drag himself out of it and then the bag changed everything. He knew finding the bag hadn't only changed his life, but it had given his life a new energy and thirst to live his life, which for so long had left him. He knew there was no going back now to the old routine, no matter what happens, *'though it might be kind of weird starting a new life behind bars for a while if it all goes pear shaped'*. But one thing was for certain, he wouldn't swap finding the bag for the world as it was the biggest wakeup call he has ever had. He thought of the moment of when he first opened the bag and then when he opened the box to find the diamonds and then shaking his head at the ritual of reading every paper possible and watching every news channel for information, just in case someone had seen him running away with the bag. He smiled to himself as he knew he'd done OK with all that, but then the day he met Kath and saw her face and watched the way her lips drank the coffee from her cup and the way her eyes spoke to his, he knew the bag with all its wealth wasn't worth as much as what he found in Kath. He thought of the strange way that the bag has brought them all together and how he felt he was somehow being guided and protected with everything, especially when a thought in his mind told him to calm down whilst he was at the top of the stairs with the gun in his hand at Beth's as it felt someone else was saying that rather than him. He thought about the coincidence some more and felt his body becoming as heavy as his eyes, he closed his eyes and fell fast asleep.

22nd April

Opening his eyes, he quickly glanced at his phone. It was 6am but already his mind was thinking. He climbed out of bed, put some clothes on, and went downstairs to make a brew. Even Barney knew it was early as he stayed in his basket and just looked over at him with a little wag of the tail which was basically saying, 'am staying here, Dad'. He took a few sips of his tea and went back upstairs and sat on the edge of the bed. Somehow he felt defeated and tried to psyche himself up by saying, "Come on, Shaun, this isn't over yet!"

'Time to step up,' he thought. He opened the blinds of the windows and saw the sunlight bursting through the glass which filled him with fresh hope and optimism.

Bathroom duties complete, though the 3 S`s were only 2 today which meant he obviously didn't eat enough fibre the last few days, he quickly got changed into his suit, made brew number 2 and went into the garden with Barney. As usual, he fed the birds then sat down to drink his brew and roll up the first cig of the day. Considering the whole thing was heading into meltdown he felt an optimism inside that was growing and felt surprisingly good now, maybe it was the shower or the second brew or the cig or was it he simply he couldn't change things now and knew saving Beth and Kath was the right path for him to take, so he may as well sit back and enjoy the show as there was no turning back now. Even though he had entertained the idea of telling

176

Kath and Beth to go it alone in the last few days it was clear now that the bag that had brought them together still hadn't finished with him just yet. He smiled at the thought of the bag bringing them all together and, once again, thought that maybe other forces were working behind the scenes somewhere and as a result there may be more than just a glimmer of hope and they would be OK, as maybe he didn't find the bag at all but the bag had found him! He lit up another cig and tended to his plants and stood there motionless for a few seconds and said, "God help me, for what am going to do."

He called Kath on the phone and asked if Beth got the boss's number and Kath gave him all the details, "What you going to do, Shaun, with them, or is it best I don't know?"

"Am going to do the right thing, Kath, as I have thought of a new plan and am going to look after you both, so don't worry about a thing. I have to get to work now so will talk to you later, babe."

"OK, Shaun, drive safe and talk later."

As he put the phone down he thought to himself, *'a new plan! Geez, it's called suicide, but what the hell'*.

He took Barney out for a walk and on getting back he quickly fed him and then fired up the car and drove to work. He stopped off at the Tesco garage on the way for some fuel, a coffee and a croissant. Whilst at the lights he looked at a man getting into a taxi with a holdall bag very similar to the one he found, *'Christ's sake, Shaun, look away,'* he thought, *'as you don't want to get involved in another bag'*. The croissant was doing its thing this morning, as bits were flaking off onto his suit and the floor, but today he wasn't bothered and just took a few extra slurps of his coffee to wash it down. Lighting up a cig to finish off the car breakfast made the journey that morning complete.

As soon as he walked into the office he said his good mornings and said to Katie that he had to have the day off tomorrow as he needed to go the dentist to get his back tooth looked at as it's giving him grief.

"Yeah, OK, Shaun, no problem, but what about the meeting tomorrow afternoon?"

"Ohh, just give my apologies and let me have the minutes when you do them, as I cannot let this toothache continue as I have been up all night with the damn thing."

"Have you took anything for it, Shaun?"

"Oh, you name it, I've taken it last night, am nearly high on all the painkillers I've taken."

"Oh, OK, well, just make sure you have intervals of 4 hours between the tablets you take."

"OK, thanks doctor," he said and the 2 of them grinned.

A few bodies were missing in the office this morning and, for once, it was quite quiet.

"So, if you don't mind me asking, Shaun, how's your new girlfriend?"

"Oh, she is amazing, it's unreal the way it is."

"Oh, so she has sorted the stuff out now with her daughter?"

"Yeah, all sorted that Katie."

"Am glad, Shaun, I just wish I could find someone amazing too."

"Am sure you will, Katie, as you certainly deserve to."

"Ahh, thanks Shaun."

"You putting the kettle on now, Katie?"

"Hmm, I was wondering why you was being nice to me!" she laughed.

Midday soon came around and Kath gave him a quick call to see how he was. He mentioned to Kath to make sure Beth didn't do anything herself and if any further calls from Craig, she must call him.

"OK, Shaun, but I must go now as I have to go back to the office," she said.

"OK lovely, well, you have a good day and I will catch you later."

Shaun stared at the name and number of Paul's and Craig's boss that Kath had just given him and sat there deep in thought for a few minutes. He then headed back to the office and finished the work he was doing and asked Katie if she fancied a coffee.

"Sorry, Shaun, if I don't get this work done by 4 o'clock today, then there will be trouble."

"OK kid, no worries, am just going to nip down the cafe and grab a coffee myself, cya soon."

Rather than walk to the normal cafe they went to, he decided to go to the Costa store in the town centre where he met Kath. He ordered his latte and, as he did, he looked at the table outside where he met Kath and let some warm thoughts run through his mind. When he was served he took his coffee outside and sat himself down, the table where he had met Kath was now occupied by some other couple, they seemed happy as they shared banter and laughter together and that brought a smile to his face. He sipped his latte and wondered what was the best way to speak to Paul's boss in the police special unit. Eventually he finished his latte, walked across to some phone booths, dialled the number in and waited for the phone to be picked up.

"Hello, Steve Hodges."

"Oh, err, hiya Steve, am wondering whether you may be interested in a story I have."

"Who's this?" he replied.

"Let's just say am no one, but I've come across something that is getting out of control and someone is likely to get seriously hurt."

"Can I ask why you're calling me?" said Steve, "as you need to call 999."

"Well, let's just say Steve it concerns one of your team and its connected to some shootings a few weeks ago."

There was a brief silence and Steve then replied, "Hmm, OK, so how do I meet you?"

"Steve, am prepared to tell you this story and am placing all my trust in you, so will you come alone and promise not to arrest me and you must also promise that you must not mention this to anyone in your squad as someone is giving out information from your circle!"

Steve replied by saying, "Is this a wind up, mate?"

"Steve can you meet me in Caffè Nero in Lime St Station at 5? Well? Can you do that Steve?"

"OK. I will meet you there, how will I recognise you?"

Shaun replied by saying, "I will be sitting there on my own reading the paper."

"OK then, see you at 5," said Steve.

Shaun put the phone down, he could feel his heart banging in his chest, *'this is it,'* he thought and headed back to work.

"You took your time getting back," said Katie.

"Yeah, I met an old mate in town and had a chat."

"How's your tooth now, Shaun?"

"Oh, it's a nightmare, kid."

Katie just looked at him with that 'I know you're lying through your back teeth' look but said nothing else. He then texted Kath and said he had arranged to meet up with Paul's boss and he will let her know one way or another later tonight.

The rest of the afternoon at work seemed to take an age to pass and Shaun's mind was conjuring up all sorts of scenarios in his mind on how the meet may go, knowing this could be disastrous for him too.

"Well, that's my lot for today," said Katie, "I managed to get the whole thing done, and if am lucky, I will be able to pick my daughter up on time today! Are you going now, Shaun?"

"Err, no, I've a few things I need to do."

"Oh, OK then, Shaun. Ta-ra and good luck at the dentist tomorrow."

"Thanks, Katie."

He made himself a brew and asked Andy if he wanted a brew too, "No, it's OK mate, am getting off myself in a minute, but thanks, mate."

He sat down at his desk, looking at the clock, and it felt like he was waiting for the electric chair as every minute that passed he felt an anxiousness growing deeper inside him.

"Well, am off now," said Andy, "you sure you're OK, Shaun?"

"Let's just say, hopefully, I will be able to tell you everything next week."

Andy looked at Shaun with a confused look, "Next week? I cannot wait till next week!"

"Well, this time, Andy, am afraid you're going to have to wait, but it will be worth the wait one way or another!"

Andy said something in his thick Wigan accent which just went straight over Shaun's head, *'but am sure it was good, whatever he said, as he was smiling as he said it'*. He would often upset Andy by calling him a Wigan pie eating git and he always replied he was from Ashton and proud of it, but to Shaun, Wigan and Ashton were the same place. But today he looked at Andy and said, "Listen, mate, you have a good night you Ashton pie eating git and I will see you next week."

He was now alone in the office and he had 40 minutes to wait, he decided to lock up the office and go outside the building and smoke a few thousand cigarettes to calm his anxiety. As he switched his laptop off he looked at the picture of his mum and his grandson on his desk and left the office.

He headed for Lime St Station and stood outside having a cig, he could see Caffè Nero from where he was standing. A few people were sitting down and having a coffee but no one looked like they were in the police, checking his watch it was 16:45 so he went to the newsagents in the station to buy a paper and headed back to Caffè Nero. His nerves were now at breaking point and he went back outside and lit yet another cig up and pulled hard on it and, as he did, he noticed a man walking towards Caffè Nero, a big strong man who you wouldn't want to mess with by the looks of him but he turned around and walked across to the ticket office. Throwing his cig to the ground he went to Caffè Nero, ordered 2 lattes, and took a chair next to the high glass walls of the station where he had a good vantage point as he could see every entrance and exit point. He opened the paper and sat there looking around, then totally out of nowhere a man as plain as hell sat down next to him.

"So, you got a story to tell?"

"Are you Steve?"

"Yep, I am."

"Well, I got you a coffee, Steve, as we may be here some time."

"And your name is?" asked Steve.

"Oh, my name is Shaun.

"OK Shaun, fire away."

Shaun told him the story of walking his dog that day and Steve sat there intrigued by what he was hearing but never said a word he just listened. Shaun explained about the finding of the bag and the diamonds and the gun but left out mentioning the money. Steve sipped his coffee and shook his head when Shaun told him of the chance meeting with Kath and Steve muttered his first word, "Unreal."

He then told him about Beth and all the happenings with her and the threats from the gang and Craig, then mentioned the meet tomorrow night with Craig and all that led up to that, "And that's where am up to right now to this moment," said Shaun.

Steve looked at Shaun and said, "Yes, I get it with the diamonds as anyone who found them may be tempted to run with them, but meeting up with the people connected with them? Am struggling with it as the coincidence is unbelievable, yet I do believe you. But you could have got yourself killed and everyone else around you with what happened after it. Just for curiosity, have you still got the diamonds?"

"Yeah, I still got them, I have even considered taking them to the bank where they came from and simply giving them back."

Steve looked at Shaun and said, "Well, that would be different!"

Steve stood up and Shaun looked up at him and said, "Are you going to arrest me now?"

Steve looked at him very sternly and then said, "No. I've finished my coffee and need another one after that story, same again, Shaun?"

"Err, yeah please."

Shaun felt the relief run threw his body and looked at Steve whilst he was at the counter, he was probably in his mid-thirties and quite well built, in fact, he had the air of a soldier about him for some strange reason he thought.

'Maybe it was the way he spoke and his mannerisms and a stern look to make you shit yourself'.

Steve placed another 2 coffees on the table and said, "OK, Shaun, now tell me it all again, and don't miss anything out at all."

He set away telling Steve everything from day one and also telling him how he felt for Kath and how he covered the fact he had the diamonds. When he got around to the part of telling him about the day he went around to the house with a Glock 19 handgun in his jacket Steve just shook his head and said, "Madness."

Shaun didn't miss anything out, from checking the news and the papers every day to Kath and Beth and then the meet with Craig and how he managed to get Craig to own up to his actions that night of the shooting.

"We seem to have a situation here Shaun and I hope you realise you're in this up to your ears?"

"Yeah, I do, Steve, but my life was rubbish before I found the bag and it made me feel alive again. But I didn't think in a million years I would meet the mum of the daughter whose partner was killed trying to get them diamonds."

"So, Shaun, you saying you're telling me all this for love?"

"Yes, I guess I am, Steve, but I think am doing it for me too as am not a bad man, Steve. I just simply had a dream of a new life."

"Well, a new life in prison, seems to me, Shaun."

"Yeah, but if it means Kath and Beth are safe, then I guess God may judge me differently than you. I've even written a letter for Kath explaining it all in case I do get arrested as I would like her to understand what I've done."

Steve took a sip of his coffee and told Shaun that he lost his wife 3 years ago due to cancer, "It was a terrible ordeal," he said, "and the way your life was shit, Shaun, I've been there too. A few years of walking 'round in a world of hurt and loneliness but just never been lucky enough to meet someone in the way you have, am just married to my job now, but one day you never know!"

"Well, it took me by surprise, Steve. From zero to hero in a blink of an eye."

"Did you really think about walking into the bank in London, Shaun, and handing them diamonds back over?"

"Yeah, I did Steve, nuts I know, but that's what I was thinking of doing. As for the love of money I couldn't just throw them away or take a chance and hand them to the police, but in a strange way, Steve, I think Paul is making all this happen, as am convinced other forces are working behind the scenes on this as the odds on me finding a bag of diamonds, then keeping hold of them, then finding Kath etc. the odds on it I couldn't calculate but it all seems to have a purpose."

Steve just stared at Shaun and said, "Well, if you say what's happened is 100% accurate, then yes, I agree it's strange, but it's not over yet! Thing is Shaun, Craig has been under suspicion for a lot of things for a long time and we suspected he may be involved in the shootings etc. In fact, the whole thing, but we cannot pin him down to anything and no one is saying a word against him too."

"If you don't mind me saying, Steve, why the hell have you got him as a undercover cop then if that's the case?"

"Proof, Shaun, you need proof."

"Well, how about Stanley Park tomorrow at 10:30 then?"

Steve stared at Shaun and you could see that he was thinking it over in his mind, "Can I meet Beth?"

"Yeah, that's not a problem, she should be home now."

"Well you better come with me then," said Steve.

"Listen, Steve, maybe it might be best if you came with me and let me drive. As, I know this might sound crazy, but if Craig is watching the house and sees your car and recognises you, then game over. Why don't I drive you there and maybe meet at her mum's house?"

"OK Shaun, let's play it your way."

Shaun called Kath and told her to get Beth at her house in 30 minutes, "Oh, OK Shaun, I will tell her to come over straight away. Is there anything up Shaun?"

"Err, kind of, Kath, but don't worry, I will see you soon."

They walked across to the car park where Shaun's car was, and as they did he told Steve of the endless hours of watching the news and reading every paper to get all the info he needed, and even spoke of the man in the shop selling all the sandwiches to the police who gave him more info than any news channel.

"I think you're wasting your time in your job," remarked Steve, "you should have been a copper too, you would make a good detective."

"Oh, I don't know about that, Steve. Listen, Steve, tell me more about your wife, how long were you together?"

You could see that Steve still missed his wife and the love for her was still strong when he briefly spoke about her earlier. He told Shaun all about her and how he still finds himself talking to her some nights, "You're the first person I've ever told that too, Shaun."

"Well, maybe you need to talk more about her to others too as it's a good thing to talk about your feelings and loved ones. Then maybe you may be able to move on better and still hold them in your heart too."

As he finished talking they arrived at Kath's and he pulled the car up outside. Kath opened the door and they both walked in, Shaun explained who Steve was to Kath and, as Kath went upstairs to get Beth, Shaun quietly said to Steve, "Please don't mention I have the diamonds."

Beth came down the stairs and instantly said hello to Steve as they had met briefly at the funeral. They walked into the living room and sat down.

Steve said to Beth, "OK, from the phone call from Paul that night right through till now, tell me everything that has happened."

Steve asked Kath for some paper and started to write everything down. Beth told him everything, from Paul and the 3 men gang that came round to the house and all about Craig and the trip to London and the meet she had and the phone call to arrange another meet tomorrow night. She told Steve how she had tricked Craig into admitting he had a lot to do with it and he was definitely there the night Paul died, and how he told her to keep her mouth shut about him at the funeral about the 3 day trip to London and that he had sorted it out with the gang but they still want to meet her tomorrow night. Steve sat back and asked if there was any chance of a cup of tea.

Kath quickly went out to put the kettle on and within a few minutes she had brought the tea in along with some biscuits.

"Listen, am going to take all this back to the office tomorrow and speak to a few guys who I can trust in the team and talk it through with them. In the meantime, don't do anything else and if Craig calls, tell him you're still going to attend the meeting or, if he has anything else to say, then just let me know as soon as possible. Right then, Shaun, you're driving me back to my car as am tired and need something to eat."

It was now 9pm and the time had just flown by.

"So, what do you think Steve?"

"Well, sounds like tomorrow is going to be a tricky day. The hard part is getting my bosses to buy into this and, as for you Shaun, am not promising anything but I will see what I can do."

"Fair enough Steve."

"Just do me a big favour, Shaun, and don't touch or go near that gun you got!"

"OK! Will do Steve."

Steve walked over to Beth and said some comforting words to her, and whatever he said seemed to help her as she smiled and thanked him.

They got into the car and Shaun drove him back towards Lime St Station to pick up his own car. As they got there, Steve got out the car and said, "Listen, I will call you tomorrow and let you know what's happening, make sure you keep your phone on at all times."

"OK, Steve, cya soon."

Shaun drove home knowing he had done the right thing and felt that Steve was a good man and, more importantly, he didn't get arrested by him. He drove to his favourite place, McDonald's, and ordered a big mac meal with a latte and sat in the car park he knew so well and ate his meal. He sat there, thinking that maybe he needs to move the money, as no doubt Steve will want to see the diamonds or some officers will call around to get them. He rolled up a cig and sat back in his car and called Kath,

"Hiya baby, I've dropped Steve off, just on my way home. All OK there?"

"Yeah, all good thanks, Shaun, and am so happy that the police are looking in to it now and Beth is happy too. He seems a nice man, that Steve."

"Yeah, he seems to be, Kath. Well, he certainly listened to what both me and Beth told him, and it seems to be agreed that Craig is one bad man. From what he told me earlier it seemed only a matter of time before they would catch up with him, but this will certainly finish him, well, hopefully."

"Well, Shaun, I can tell you that I've never been so scared in all my life of late."

"Hey, me too, Kath, it's been a crazy time indeed. Listen, babe, you spend some quality time with Beth and am going to head off home and get some quality sleep as am destroyed."

"OK, Shaun, sleep well my lovely man,"

"You too baby," and he blew her a kiss down the phone before hanging up.

As soon as he got home he was met by Barney who must have had every leg crossed as the second he opened the door he ran out and cocked his leg up against the big flower pot outside and took an age to finish too, "Good boy, son, am sorry am so late."

He clipped the lead on Barney and took him for an extra-long walk this evening and, considering he had been on the go all day and the meet up with Steve, he still felt quite good, and so much more relaxed than earlier in the day.

On getting back home he went into the loft, took out the diamonds and the gun and put them in a separate bag, then crouched down to crawl all the way into the corner of the loft and put the money there, so it was totally out of view and hard to get to. Which he knew was probably pointless, as he knew if the police searched the place, they would find it, *'but it's out of view for now,'* he thought.

He then came down the stairs and made a brew and thought about the day he had. As he did, a tiredness came over him and, as he was about to lock up and go to bed, his phone burst to life!

It was Steve, "Hi Shaun, I've made a few calls and things are in motion for tomorrow. We will be meeting Beth in the morning to go through things with her and later too, so if you want to be there, then that's fine. Oh, and Shaun, I've been thinking and, as long as all goes well tomorrow and you hand the diamonds back and the bloody gun to me, then maybe we can all forget about the day you took your dog for a walk on the railway that afternoon!"

"Thanks, Steve, thanks very much."

"OK Shaun, see you tomorrow morning about 10ish."

"OK Steve, cya then."

The phone went down and he sat there with a big smile on his face, "Fucking hell!" he shouted out loudly and punched the air in delight, "Yes, get in there!" he cried out loud again.

He turned out the lights and went to bed and said a small prayer to God, thanking him for his help and guidance in all of this and meeting Steve who was a good man and asked if it would be possible for him to find a new love as he is alone and hurting and also to look after Kath and Beth tomorrow night. He didn't manage to say anything else as he fell fast asleep and didn't even hear Barney creep up the stairs and jump on the bottom of the bed with him and they both slept soundly this night.

23rd April

Thursday

Shaun's eyes slowly opened and he reached over to his phone, *'geez, its only 06:50, I cannot sleep in even if I want to'*. He felt a heavy weight on his legs and looked down to see Barney at the end of the bed, "Hey you, who told you to come up here?"

Barney's tail was wagging nervously as he knew he doesn't sleep on the bed, but today he called Barney up to him and patted him on the head and said, "Just this once, mate, just this once."

Barney then went into overdrive by throwing himself onto his back and trying to catch his own tail, "Yeah, daft bugger, Barney. Now, come on, let's go down."

He got out of bed, put some clothes on, had a quick visit to the bathroom, then straight down the stairs to get the kettle going. Barney came down the stairs and he put Barnes in the garden whilst he brewed up. He brought his tea into the garden, sat there, and sipped his tea whilst rolling the first cig of the day. He lit up the cig and thought that this could be the day that he has wished for, to be home free to live the dream he thought had died. His mind then thought of Kath and Beth and knew that this could all go wrong in a flash. He knew Kath would be up so he sent her a text saying: ***"Morning baby how's my lovely woman today?."*** He didn't have to wait to long for a reply saying: ***"Hey sweetheart, I'm OK thanks but worried about tonight. I will call you in 10 mins x."***

He quickly made another brew and his phone went off, "Hiya hon, listen, don't worry about tonight as this team of police that are going in tonight know their stuff and can handle these types of situations really well."

"I know, Shaun, I just don't want Beth to get hurt before the police can act."

"Listen, these guys are not the ordinary police and they will make sure nothing happens to her, it will be OK."

"I've took today and tomorrow off work, Shaun, as I cannot concentrate on a thing and I will be needed to look after the kids."

"Yeah, good thinking Kath."

"Steve seemed a very caring man, didn't he, Shaun?"

"Yeah, he is. He called me again last night, he wants a good result for everyone involved babe, including his team. He told me all about his wife who died 3 years ago, she had cancer and he told me of all his struggles since then. He just opened up when I spoke to him of how we met etc."

"Aahh, the poor man," Kath replied, "she must have been very young when she died as he is only in his thirties."

"Yeah, it's a horrible thing, cancer."

"What made you tell him how we met, Shaun?"

"Err, well, he asked how long we been together so I just told him and told him a bit about my life. So maybe that's why he opened up to me too, though I did miss one thing out, Kath."

"Oh, and what was that, Shaun?"

"I didn't tell him I drugged your coffee!"

"You're a menace, Shaun," she laughed. "Listen, Kath, I will call around about 11 this morning, if that's OK, as that will give Steve and his team some time with Beth before I get there."

"Yeah, Shaun, please do."

"OK, kid, catch you after."

He quickly went back inside the house and proceeded to the bathroom for the 3 S`s and, as the water hit down hard on him in the shower, he knew only fate would decide if today was going to make or break them all. He stayed longer in the shower this morning and let the hot water do its magic against his body and enjoyed the moment as the water refreshed his mind and soul.

He threw on a pair of jeans and a top and tried his best to find a pair of socks without a bloody hole in them, *'geez, I need to throw all these old socks away,'* he thought, but eventually found a good pair and put them on.

Throwing his shoes on, he clipped the lead around Barney and took him for a morning walk. He bumped into the old lady walking her dog and she asked him where he had been as she hadn't seen him or Barney for a while. He told her that he has been walking Barney just as much as normal but at slightly different times.

"I've noticed your car not on the drive too."

'Geez, who needs neighbourhood watch when you have this woman?' he thought. "Oh, I have been seeing a lady friend."

"Oh, that's nice," she said, "is she from this estate too?"

"No, not from this estate, it's only early days yet but she is nice."

The old lady then went off on one, telling him all about her boyfriend's when she was younger and all he could do was nod his head and agree with her.

"Listen, I have to get going now as I have somewhere to go later."

"OK," she said and said goodbye to Barney.

'The whole estate will know now that the man in number 50 has got a new girlfriend in the next few hours but if it makes them happy then let them talk'. Shaun smiled as he thought, *'thank God, she wasn't the man on the roof of his shed the day I found the bag or I would have been caught within minutes as she didn't miss a trick!'* His thoughts then moved quickly to the meeting tonight and tried to imagine how it would all come off.

On getting back home, he fed Barney, then threw some bread in the toaster for himself and made a fresh brew. He took his tea and toast out into the garden, it was now 9am but he knew all he could do now was wait. He ate his toast and had a cig with his tea, then pottered around the garden tending to his plants that were starting to come up nice, now that some warmer weather was on its way, and some of his seedlings were coming up strong. He then took to the lawnmower and did the front and back garden and his mind was locked deep in thought throughout the whole lot of it but it helped kill the time. He made a fresh brew when he finished and sat back and admired the garden and his handiwork.

He went for a quick wash, then straight back into the bedroom and he went through all the drawers with his socks in and threw out all the ones he didn't want. He thought he would have a trip to Tesco to buy some new ones and get some fresh tiger bread, some ham and a shedload of cakes for the police when they came around to Kath's today.

He drove to Kath's after picking up the shopping and she met him on the driveway when he got there.

"Hey, hello you," she said and gave him a big hug, "so, what's in the bags?"

"Oh, just brought some tiger bread, ham and some cakes for our police friends."

She laughed and said, "Well, you better put them next to the stuff I've bought too."

He looked in the kitchen to see a mound of freshly cut sandwiches, "Oh well, let's hope they're all starving, eh?" he said and laughed, "If a cuppa is going now, I might even have a butty myself as am getting hungry looking at all them sandwiches!"

"Any excuse for a cup of tea for you Shaun, isn't it?"

"Yeah, I guess so babe."

As he was waiting for his tea Beth walked in and said hello and mentioned that Steve had been here earlier and it was all good to go for tonight. "Steve will be back later and some of his team will be staying all day with me in case anything else crops up."

"Well, that sounds good, Beth," he said.

"My mum was telling me all about Steve, he seems a good bloke."

"Yeah, he is, Beth, or at least he seems to be."

"Well, let's hope he is bloody good at his job," quipped Beth, "otherwise its curtains for me tonight!"

"Am sure he will get it all right, Beth, and you will be just fine."

It was a beautiful day today, with the sun bursting through the few clouds that were remaining, and they sat in the garden and discussed what was said earlier with Steve and the team.

"Listen, Mum, if anything does happen to me, you will be OK with the kids, won't you?"

"Hey, Beth, nothing like that is going to happen," said Shaun.

"Yeah, I know, but you just never know," said Beth.

Kath reassured her and said, "You know I will look after the kids, but like Shaun said, it will be fine, honey."

Shaun could see Beth was clearly getting upset and said, "Listen, Beth, your mum has me as long as she wants me and I will do my bit to make sure the kids and your mum are OK."

Beth smiled at him and Kath grasped Shaun's hand and squeezed it affectionately. The moment was broken by the sound of the doorbell and Kath went to open the door.

In walked Steve and 4 other men, they sat down in the living room and Kath offered them all tea and coffee, all of them quickly took up the offer, and then Steve introduced the team to Beth. Shaun sat there just taking it all in and listening to every word being spoken. Kath then came in with the tea and coffee for them all and brought in the sandwiches and, geez, could these guys eat as the sandwiches were demolished in minutes.

Steve said, "There has been a slight change to our plan and we want to run things by you again, Beth," and they went about telling her what she needed to do, "the team will all be watching, but out of sight, only to be seen when needed. Park your car about 30 feet away from his car if he is already there and stay in the car, let him come over to you. You will be wearing a listening device so we will hear everything that's said. But if he isn't there when you arrive, then park your car at the top right hand side of the car park, next to the entrance to the park itself, and wait in the car with your lights on."

Beth then said, "What if he tries to drive off with me?"

"He will not get past the gates, Beth, so don't worry, I can assure you that."

They told Beth things to ask Craig when he spoke to her, so hopefully they could find out more and most importantly get it all down as evidence. Shaun knew by telling Beth the other day to mention to Craig that Paul said something else to her that he had unlocked Craig's fears of being caught and the team believe he was there that night too.

After about an hour they all got up and left the house, but not before saying that some other people will be coming around the house later to set up the listening device etc. Steve lifted Beth's face gently with his hands, looked at her, and said, "Don't worry, we will have this guy and you will be OK Beth."

They all left and Kath said, "Well, what now?"

"We just wait, babe," said Shaun, "as there isn't anything else we can do."

Beth looked at her mum and said, "From what they told me they think that bastard may have even killed Paul himself! And if he did I hope, not only do they get him, but he rots in jail for the rest of his life for what he has done and for threatening me and the kids!"

"Yeah, Beth, he is one nasty little bastard," Shaun replied.

Kath then told Beth that she will pick the kids up from nursery and school later and not to worry about a thing.

"Am going to get off for a while now," said Shaun and said goodbye to Beth and walked towards the door.

Kath pulled him back and said, "When you told Beth before that you would help out with the kids if anything should go wrong and you would be with me for as long as I wanted you? Well, Shaun, I want to keep you forever as am totally yours, babe."

He gazed into her eyes, then kissed her gently and said, "Me too, honey, am all yours, guess I won't need to drug your coffee anymore then!"

She laughed and said, "Go on with yeah, get home," and blew him a kiss as he stepped into his car.

It was hard to say how he was feeling at this moment as he knew it could all go seriously wrong tonight and, as much as he wanted to let his heart sing knowing that Kath loves him, he had to keep this feeling to one side now and just prayed all went well tonight.

When he got home he decided to go into the loft and have another look at the diamonds. They sparkled like never before as the sunlight hit them through the window, he took an age admiring their beauty and he could see why some people loved diamonds. He put them back in their box, placed them back in the loft, stared over to where the money was hidden and then looked at the big holdall bag. He sat on the edge of the loft just looking at the bag and then said, "If you're listening, Paul, then everything is going OK mate, as your team are going to take Craig out tonight and Beth will be safe. So you got just a few more hours to do your stuff up there, Paul."

He got down from the loft and closed the hatch, he really did feel he was being guided through all of this and if he was, then there was nothing wrong in acknowledging this to Paul's spirit. His phone burst to life and it was Katie from work,

"Hiya Katie, what's up?"

"Am just calling to see how it went at the dentist with your bad tooth?"

"Oh, err, err, well, Katie there isn't anything wrong with my tooth, I was lying yesterday."

"I knew it," she said, "and that's why I am calling you today, are you OK, Shaun? As you're so different of late and Andy said he is concerned too."

Shaun knew Katie cared about him and he didn't want to tell her lies and said, "Listen, Katie, you're going to have to bear with me on this, but yes, something is wrong, in fact, very wrong but am hoping it's all going to be sorted one way or another today. That's all I can say for now, and if all goes well, then next week I will be able to tell you everything."

"Shaun, we're worried. Bloody hell man, you're like a dad to me and I can see it written all over your face something is not right with you, you're not ill are you?"

"No, am not ill, Katie. Am just involved up to my neck in some heavy shit which is about to come to an end today, hopefully."

"Well, you promise to call me tomorrow, Shaun?"

"Yes, I will call you, and thanks very much for making me feel ancient with the dad thing."

"Ha ha, you're welcome," she said, "though you're probably old enough to be my granddad so you should feel lucky I only said dad!"

"Yeah, OK Katie, enough said now," he said and he thanked her for the call and promised to call her tomorrow and put the phone down.

He thought about her call and remembered all the times he felt lonely and in despair due to his marriage breakdown and all the times she helped pick him up from the floor and made him think straight again. She was an absolute star, he could hide things from his own kids as they didn't see him every day, but he couldn't hide nothing from Katie and his work mates. He used to feel so alone at first when his marriage broke down but his work mates had his back all the time. He then thought about his own kids and what they would think if he ended up going to prison, *'geez, am not even going down that route,'* he thought to himself, jumped up and went to make a brew. He just knew that he had great kids and great friends who really cared about him and, when push came to the shove, they stepped in to help.

He went into the garden to drink his brew, lit up a cig and cleared his mind. Time was inching closer and he called Kath to say he would come around when the kids go to bed at seven thirty.

The tension was now building up and he decided to take Barney for a quick walk. He felt slightly out of breath as he walked Barney and knew he was stressed to the max. He shook his arms about to ease the tightening muscles in his chest and clicked his neck by moving his head side to side very quickly, which always resulted in a loud crack of the bones in his neck, which somehow always seemed to manage to ease the tension.

On getting back home he opted for a can of coke rather than a brew and the cold drink hit the spot. He went back into the garden, lit up a cig and decided to call his son.

He chatted to his son and asked what he was up to of late and suggested going into town on Saturday for some CD`s to which he replied, "Yeah, cool, Dad."

"OK then, son, will call you about 12 on Sat. Ta-ra, son."

He then called his 2 daughters and had a good chat to them both as he knew the next time he talked to them it could possibly be from a prison cell if it all went wrong. He wanted to tell them so much what was wrong, especially his son, but he couldn't as he had to protect their feelings too right now. Looking at his watch it was nearly 7pm, *'time for a quick wash and freshen up and then round to Kath's'*.

He got himself sorted and gave Barney some food, then fired up the car and went around to Kath's.

He pulled up outside, walked to the door and was met by Kath, "Phew, this is hell, babe," she said to him, "am a bag of nerves."

"Yeah, am tense too, babe, but its Beth who is going through it most at the moment. Talking of Beth where is she, Kath?"

"Oh, she is upstairs telling the kids a story."

Shaun smiled and said how he had loved telling his children stories when they were younger, "I used to make all my own stories up."

"I used to tell Beth my own stories too," replied Kath, "oh how simple it was then, when they're all young and innocent, and this mad old world hadn't caught up with them then."

"I hear you, babe, but it's the stories that help the kids decide what's good and bad and prepare them for the world. So my kids would be well and truly prepared with some of the stories I told them!" he let out a big laugh, "Geez, I used to scare them to death with some of the stories, but then some stories I told them made them think of others and to look out for the weak ones and protect them, great days them."

"You fancy a cig outside, Shaun?"

"Yeah, why not, babe."

"I've never smoked so many cigs in my life as of late, Shaun."

"Me too, babe. If I didn't smoke, I wouldn't like to guess how many fingers I would have chewed off by now!"

They had their cigs and were joined by Beth, "They're both fast asleep now."

"That's good," said Kath.

"I told them the story of the gingerbread man, not once but twice, they love that story."

Beth's phone went off and Shaun and Kath immediately went silent as they listened, "Oh, OK Steve, thanks," she said and put the phone down, "the men are coming 'round to fit me with a listening device in a few minutes, phew this is it then, eh?"

"You just do as they say, Beth, and it will be OK, babe."

A few seconds of silence filled the air as the tension built up. Shaun tried to defuse the situation by saying, "It's amazing all the high-tech gadgets they have now, and they're so small you wouldn't believe that they could do that."

As he finished talking the doorbell went and 2 guys in plain clothes walked in. They explained what they were going to do and how it worked to Beth, and besides a listening device they were also placing a tracker on the car, just in case.

Beth got changed into some different clothes and then came down and let the men place the listening device on her and then they set about sorting the car out. They then checked the equipment and when they were happy with it all, Beth's phone got a text and it was a message from Craig. It simply said: ***Be there at 10:30 sharp!***" She told the 2 plain clothes men about the text she just received and they called it in and said,

"It's a definite go for tonight."

Time seemed to stand still for the next hour or so and it was now nearly 10 o'clock. Beth was trying her best to remain calm but her mum was in bits.

"Listen, Kath, try to be strong for Beth. Don't let her see you like this as it will only make her more anxious."

"I will try, Shaun," she wiped her runny nose and eyes and gave him a hug.

Beth came over and said, "Mum, don't worry, as soon as I get away from Craig I will call you."

Shaun's phone went off and it was Steve, "Listen, Shaun, everything is good to go up here. Tell Beth she is in good hands."

"I will Steve, good luck mate," Shaun told Beth that, "Steve said all was good and for you not to worry."

She smiled and said, "Well, I think I will have one more cig before we do it."

They all went into the garden and lit up a cig. Beth appeared to be the strongest of them all and said, "Don't worry you two, I will be back in half an hour and you can make me cuppa and some toast Mum."

"Yes, you will," said Shaun, "and I will make you that toast as well."

The two police guys did one last check of the listening device and said, "It's time! Just remember to ask what we told you and if you see if he is carrying a weapon then somehow try to let us know what it is, so we know what we are up against."

"I will," she replied, "am ready."

She walked towards the door, turned around and gave her mum a hug, then headed off to her car and drove off without even looking around.

"She seemed determined to me, Kath, and full of confidence."

"Yeah, she did. She is a brave girl and always has been, even at school she wouldn't allow anyone to bully her and would deal with them promptly."

One of the officers said, "Listen guys, we have to get going too, we will let you know when it's all over."

"Thanks, lads, and good luck," said Shaun.

The officer looked over to Kath and said, "Don't worry missus, she will be fine," and then said, "incidentally, there is a few more of us outside your house too in case there is a change of plan, so don't worry on all fronts," and they then went on their way.

Kath cried and he held her in his arms, "Come on babe, let's have a coffee and sit outside."

He made her a coffee and brought it out and they sat there drinking the coffee. Kath was checking her phone every few seconds, "Hey, Kath, your phone is working. Now, come on, let's try to calm ourselves and think positive here. In fact, tell me more about them stories you used to tell Beth as a child."

Kath started to tell him all about Beth as a kid and some of the stories she used to love telling. He would prompt her on some things, just to make sure she would carry on talking to stop her from worrying.

Beth had now reached Stanley Park and headed for the gates to the huge car park. This car park would be full on match days for Liverpool and Everton, and in-between matches it would be used as 2 full size football pitches, but tonight there wasn't one car in sight. It was dark now and she entered the gates and drove up to the far right at the top of the car park. She turned the car around to face the gates in the distance and switched her engine off but kept the lights on. Her hands were shaking as she fumbled with her fingers to try and light up a cigarette to help control her nerves. She looked at the clock on the dashboard, it was 10:27, and she could feel her heart beating in her chest. She pulled hard on her cigarette as she looked all around her but nothing or no one in sight.

Meanwhile Shaun was looking at his watch and even though he wasn't there his stomach was in knots. He went to the bathroom to throw some water on his face, looked in the mirror, stared at his own reflection and tried to get himself together before walking back down the stairs to Kath.

Beth flicked her cig out the window and looked again at the time, it was now 10:30. The car park was now pitch black, except for the area her headlights were lighting up and she felt she was starting to lose it. Beth was not a normally a chain smoker but lit up another cig and, as she lit the cig, she looked at the clock on the dashboard and it was now 10:34. She then noticed a light at the bottom gate and stared straight at it and it was clear that it was headlights on what looked like a white van. It pulled up about 10 feet away from her, she could now see Craig behind the wheel. He looked over at her and shouted over for her to get out the car. She shouted back out from her dropped window,

"What for, where you taking me?"

Craig said, "Am taking you to meet them."

"No," she shouted, "you said the meet was here and am not going anywhere in that van."

Craig jumped out the van, opened the back doors and shouted at her to get out the fucking car and get in the van,

"No, am staying here," she said.

Craig walked over and opened her door, then dragged her out the car by her hair, "You're as fucking dumb as Paul, now get in the van," he said and pushed her towards the van doors.

She fell on the floor but picked herself up quickly and tried to make a run for it.

"Stop right now or I will kill you right here, you fucking bitch."

Beth stopped and noticed he had a gun and said, "You're going to shoot me, just like the way you killed Paul then, eh? It was you, wasn't it?!"

Craig looked at her and smiled, "Well, what do you expect when he fucked up the most simple of jobs? And it was my plan and I was never splitting it with him."

Beth felt the anger run through her veins and shouted back, "So it was you, you bastard!" she shouted and tried to make another run for it.

As she ran Craig fired the gun and Beth hit the floor instantly. A second shot was fired, but this time Craig was sent sprawling against the tarmac. The team came from nowhere, surrounding Craig, whilst two officers ran to Beth.

"How is she?" asked Steve.

"She's all right boss, but we better get her to hospital quickly."

"OK, call it in."

Steve walked over to where Craig lay on the floor, "No point me asking if he is OK," he commented as he stood over Craig's body with blood oozing from his head, "OK, cover him."

Steve went back over to Beth who was starting to come back around, "It's a good job you can run fast. Beth. You're going to be OK, it looks like the bullet has missed anything too serious, and we have a medical team to look after you now and they will take you the hospital. I will tell your mum to come over to the hospital later when I've sorted this mess out."

Beth muttered the words that Craig had killed Paul and did they get him,

"Yeah, we got him, Beth, he is probably explaining himself to Paul right now up there as we speak."

Beth tried to smile and then the paramedics came over and went to work on her and got her in to the ambulance.

The aftermath was all cleaned up and Craig's body taken away and Steve called Kath.

Kath nearly jumped out of the seat when the phone went off and was scared to answer the phone in case of bad news, but she put the phone to her ear and listened. Shaun looked on as Kath shouted, "How bad is she?! Oh, OK, OK."

It was clear Kath was in shock and Shaun asked to speak to Steve, "She has been shot, Shaun," said Kath as she passed him the phone.

"Hiya Steve, how is she, mate?"

"Beth has been shot, mate, but she has been taken to hospital and I think she will be OK. She took a nasty one to the top of her shoulder but, luckily, it may not have hit anything more serious. But they have taken her to the Royal Hospital, I will find out how she is and get back to you as soon as I know more."

"Thanks Steve, what has happened with Craig?"

"He is dead, Shaun, so it's over. I will speak to you more later about this, but for now I will call you as soon as I know more about Beth as am going straight to the hospital now and I should be there any minute."

"Thanks, Steve."

Shaun hugged Kath and reassured her that Beth would be fine and told her that Craig is dead so it was all over, Kath hugged him and Shaun could feel all the emotion draining out of him and he put his head on Kath's shoulders and closed his eyes and held her tight.

"You OK, Shaun?" she asked.

"Yeah, am just a bit overcome like you, Kath, as it's been so trying these last few days," Shaun was mentally exhausted with it all and felt like he was drunk, "I think I need a cup of tea or something before we go to the hospital."

"Yeah, good idea," she said.

The two of them sat outside and had their tea and a cig when the phone went and it was Steve,

"Hiya Shaun, put Kath on the phone for us please?"

"It's Steve, Kath, he wants to speak to you."

Kath took the phone and said, "Hello Steve, everything OK?"

"Yeah, all OK here, Kath. Someone wants to speak to you."

As Kath listened she heard Beth's voice say, "Hello Mum, the bastard shot me in the shoulder!"

Kath didn't know whether to laugh or cry when she heard her, "But am going to fine, Mum, so don't worry, bring me some stuff in for us, please?"

Kath instantly said, "Oh baby, am glad you're OK. I will bring some bits in for you now."

"Thanks Mum, I love you."

"I love you too, Beth, see you soon."

Steve came back on the phone and told her where to find her in the hospital and said that she was just going into surgery now to get the bullet removed but she will be fine and he was going to stay there till she gets out of surgery. Kath thanked Steve for looking after her girl,

"You're welcome, Kath."

An hour later Steve called to say she was out of surgery and all went well and if they wanted to come over now, then that's good.

"Shaun, do you mind if I go to the hospital and you look after the kids? As I don't want to wake them up and tell them their mum is in hospital right now."

"Yeah, sure, no problem at all, babe. I will just stick the tele on and cabbage on the sofa now that it's all over, give Beth a kiss for me too."

"I will Shaun, and Shaun? Am madly in love with you, you coffee drugging swine."

"So you should be too," he said, "now get yourself to hospital."

As she drove off he sat on the sofa with a huge grin on his face, he lay back on the sofa and closed his eyes and enjoyed the moment of success and happiness, and not forgetting riches, and fell asleep.

Kath came back about 5am and woke him up with a cup of tea, "Hey, hello you."

"Sorry babe, I must have nodded off."

"Yes, I could hear you snoring from outside."

"Oh dear, sorry about that, Kath."

"It's OK," she laughed.

"How's Beth?"

"She is going to be just fine, Shaun, as they say there is no major damage and, in time, she will make a full recovery. Just going to be a bit sore for a while and hopefully she will be out of hospital in a few days."

"Well, that's great news, Kath. Listen, babe, you will need to get some sleep yourself as the kids will be up in a few hours."

"You staying here too, Shaun, or you getting back home?"

"Think it's best I get home and let Barney out for a wee as he will have had all his legs crossed waiting," he laughed.

"OK, lovely, I will see you tomorrow," she said.

Shaun gave her a big hug and blew her a kiss as he got into his car and headed off home.

As soon as he got home he let Barney out into the garden for a wee and lit up a cig. When finished, he called Barney in and locked up. As Barney sat in his basket he spoke to Barney and said, "Thanks boy for finding that bag and making us rich and happy, mate," and as he turned out the downstairs light he called Barney upstairs, to which Barney flew up the stairs and jumped on to the bed, "just tonight though, Barney" he said, "for being a clever boy."

Shaun lay down in his bed and thanked God and Paul for all their help and fell asleep for a few hours till his phone alarm went off at 7am. He quickly switched it off and had another hour shut eye.

He got out of bed full of the joys of spring, considering he only slept a few hours, and hit the bathroom, then went downstairs to make a brew and sat in the garden with his brew and a cig. Seeing the world once again, but this time without any pressure. He still had to go to work today but thought he would go in for 10 o'clock and took Barney out for a morning walk.

As he walked Barney he felt so different than normal, as for the last few weeks his thoughts have been crazy and his mind totally wired, but now it's all over he felt kind of strange but in a good way, "I cannot believe it's over Barney," he said and Barney looked at him blankly.

On arrival back at home, he made another brew and sat again in the garden and had another cig when his phone went off and it was Steve.

"Hiya Steve, all OK?"

"Yeah, I thought I would drop by before I go to work this morning."

"Oh great, well, I live in number 50…"

Before he could finish saying where he lived Steve cut in and said, "Shaun, I know where you live! I am a policeman remember? That's my job!"

Shaun laughed and said, "Oh, yeah OK, well, I will see you soon then, mate."

About 15 minutes later Steve arrived at the house and had a coffee with Shaun, "So Shaun, how does it feel knowing that you probably helped saved Beth's life last night?"

"Geez, Steve, that was not me but you who saved her!"

"If you didn't call me, things may have been so different, Shaun, so you did well."

"Fair enough Steve, but you saved her though mate."

"So Shaun, the diamonds! Let's see them and see what all this fuss was about."

Shaun went upstairs into the loft and brought them down, along with the handgun.

"I think I will take the gun if you don't mind, Shaun."

"No, please do, Steve."

Shaun then opened the bag and gave Steve the box with the diamonds in and, as he opened them, he stared at them for a while and said, "The things people do for these, eh? Listen, Shaun, you do have to give them back, you know?"

"Trust me, Steve, I want to I really do."

"OK, leave it with me and I will sort it out for you to do just that."

"Thanks Steve, thanks a lot, mate."

Steve looked at Shaun and said, "Just for asking's sake, where have you hid the money?"

Shaun's face dropped, "Err, err, the money, Steve?

"Yeah, the money that Paul was carrying."

Shaun looked at Steve and said dejectedly, "It's under the floor insulation in the loft."

Steve looked at Shaun and with a grin said, "Well, I hope you're going to use some of that to take Kath and Beth and the kids on a holiday when Beth's a bit better?!"

"Yeah," said Shaun with a sigh of relief, "I will do just that."

"OK Shaun, I will call you when I sort the diamond handover out for you."

Shaun nodded his head and shook Steve's hand, "You're a good man, Steve."

"Yeah, I am," said Steve, "too bloody good!"

The Next Week

Shaun took a train to London with Steve, his own personal guard, and went to the bank. He met the manager and a few other employees of importance and then handed over the diamonds. They were overjoyed at the diamonds and they quickly pointed out to the 3 big ones. They shook Shaun's hand and gave him a reward, a cheque for 20 thousand pounds, which he accepted gracefully and then they were both taken out to lunch.

"That cheque will come in handy, Steve."

"Well, it should pay towards that holiday, Shaun."

"So Steve, how's, err, Beth? As you been seeing her every night in hospital!"

"Well, let's just say, Shaun, that things are looking up."

2 Months Later

Shaun took Kath and Beth and the kids to Disneyland in California, oh, and a certain man called Steve came to keep an eye on Beth!

'It appears the bag has looked after all of us!'